MURDER WITHOUT MOTIVE

By
R. L. GOLDMAN

●

WILDSIDE PRESS

www.wildsidepress.com

PRIZE MYSTERY
NOVELS

I T is the aim of the Publishers to bring
to the public from time to time, inex-
pensive editions of better detective mystery novels to be known as PRIZE MYS-
TERY NOVELS. They are slightly con-
densed, but only such matter not pertinent
to the plot has been eliminated.

T HIS mystery thriller is published by
Crestwood Publishing Co., Inc., by ar-
rangement with Coward-McCann, and
was originally published at $2.00.

CHAPTER 1

I HAD PLANNED to write this story in the third person so as to avoid any possible impression that I consider myself its principal character. But after writing an assortment of opening paragraphs, I gave it up as a bad job. I know my limitations.

I can chase facts and recognize them when I catch up with them, and I can write about what I know in English as unadorned with fancy trimmings as a T-bone steak at a pie-wagon. But that lets me out. The only time I was in college was when I went to interview the Chancellor of Fairmont University to find out how badly the bursar had nicked the college treasury when he ran off to South America with one of the senior co-eds.

I was with the *Times* then, and my interview scored a beat. A few weeks later, at a press dinner, I met Asaph Clume, owner and managing editor of the *Express*.

At the time when I found him sitting next to me at the press dinner, I knew him only by reputation. Although I had been in the newspaper game for six years, I was only twenty-five years old; and his immediate presence overawed me. He was a tall, lanky man of sixty, with heavy, prominent features, a wide mouth, a long nose, and deepset gray eyes. I thought he resembled Lincoln without the whiskers.

I was trying to decide whether I ought to speak to him when he reached for my place-card and squinted at it under gray, shaggy brows.

"Rufus Reed. *The Times*." He turned to look at me. "Are you the red-headed squirt who got in to see Chancellor Bellamy and interviewed him while my prize interviewer was standing outside on the campus gazing wishfully at the windows?"

I felt the customary flush breaking over me. In order to cover my confusion, I tried to speak lightly.

"I'm guilty," I said. "And are you, by chance, Mr. Asaph Clume?"

"I'm Asaph Clume," he replied solemnly, "but I don't believe it's by chance."

I was flattered by his attention. All during dinner he bombarded me with his shrewd and caustic comments about everything under the sun. With the coffee, the dignitaries at the speakers' table got into action; and for an hour Clume sat motionless with his eyes closed. When the toastmaster was introducing the last and principal speaker of the evening, Clume roused himself. The speaker was Thomas Wendell, whose only claim to being a newspaper man resided in the fact that he owned the controlling interest in the *Star-Herald*, the largest of Fairmont's three newspapers.

Thomas Wendell was around forty-five years old, of medium height and sturdy build, clean shaven and ruddy skinned, with a fleshy, bulbous nose, and large lustrous brown eyes. His broad shoulders, thick neck, and long arms gave one the impression of great physical power, an impression that was dispelled when he walked; for a leg wound received in the World War had left him with a stiffened right knee, and he limped badly.

Not long ago I had written an article about him in which I called him the Cinderella Man. That went over big, and it was really appropriate.

You see, Thomas Wendell very nearly missed being the scion, the leading, the foremost, etc., etc. He nearly missed it twice, in fact. His first narrow escape occurred before he was born. His grandfather, John Wendell, had two sons, Arnold and Paul. Arnold, the elder, was a typical Wendell; steady-going, practical, and stolid. Paul had a streak of wildness in him. He was impractical and emotionally unstable.

When Paul was in his senior year at Fairmont University, he took up with a girl the family didn't approve of — and for better reasons, I understand, than mere snobbishness. When they realized that the affair was serious, they tried to break it up. But Paul was determined to marry the girl, and marry her he did. He not only defied his father and eloped with the girl, but he took the opposition to the marriage as a personal insult which he said he didn't intend to forgive. In other words, instead of his father kicking him out, he kicked himself out. He signed away his right to inheritance for one hundred thousand dollars cash, and left Fairmont. He never returned, not even after his wife died in childbirth a year later.

In biographical sketches, this period is briefly alluded to. Paul remained alienated from his family until he died nearly thirty years later. When John Wendell died, Arnold inherited everything. Neither Paul nor his son Thomas was mentioned in the will. That was in 1912.

Thomas was about twenty-eight years old when his father died in 1917. Father and son were running a small sheep ranch in Wyoming, all that remained of the mess of pottage for which Paul had traded his birthright; and the ranch had almost as many mortgages on it as sheep. At Paul's death, Thomas inherited nothing but debts, and he gave up the last spoonful of pottage to satisfy the claims of the creditors. The bankers gave him a job as manager of the ranch he had once owned, and that's where he was, almost on his uppers, when the Cinderella theme entered his story.

Arnold, who had never married, had intended leaving his money to various charities and scientific foundations. But when Paul died, Arnold had a change of heart. His nephew, whom he had never seen, was his only relative and the last of the Wendell line. He began to question the justice of ignoring his brother's son. But before he changed his will, he made careful inquiries about Thomas; for he had no idea what sort of man he had turned out to be. The reports he received from disinterested men in Wyoming reassured him. The general opinion of Thomas was that he was an exemplary young man. Steady-going? He hadn't left his ranch in years except to attend to business in nearby Sheridan. Faithful? He had stuck to his father through thick and thin, working his head off in an effort to save the ranch. Capable? The ranch would have gone under long before it did except for Thomas' wise management. Honest? He had given up his ranch rather than let any creditor hold the bag. There was no foreclosure; he had sold out so that he could pay off his father's debts one hundred cents on the dollar.

That was enough to satisfy Arnold. He wrote to his nephew and asked him to come to Fairmont as rightful heir to the Wendell fortune.

But by that time, the United States had entered the war, and Thomas had enlisted in the army. He was in a Wyoming training camp and was just about to be shipped overseas. His coming to Fairmont was postponed, to take place under more dramatic and romantic circumstances.

Arnold died in 1918, and the Wendell fortune passed on to a young man who was fighting somewhere in France. That was how, for the second time, he very nearly missed being the Cinderella man. If the shell fragments had got him a little higher up —

The administrators of the estate found him in a Boston army hospital, informed him of his uncle's death, and crowned him king. A month later, when he was discharged from the hospital, he came to Fairmont and took hold. And I mean to say that he took hold! He made all previous Wendells look like clumsy amateurs. He inherited about a third of Fairmont and energetically set out to acquire the remaining two-thirds. Now, fourteen years later, he had just about accomplished it.

While Wendell was speaking, I glanced from time to time at Clume. He kept his deep-set eyes fixed on Wendell, his face hard with dislike. His hostility did not surprise me; everyone was aware of the antagonism of the two men. Politically, Clume and his *Express* were on one side of the fence, and Wendell and the machine were on the other. But Clume's repugnance was based on a matter more personal than political differences. Five years before, when Wendell was gaining control of the *Star* and the *Herald* — which he later merged into the present *Star-Herald* — he had tried unsuccessfully to buy out Clume's interest in the *Express*. When Clume refused to sell, Wendell resorted to various indirect means of persuasion, chiefly, I believe, through the Fairmont Trust Company, whose Board of Directors Wendell headed. I recall some talk at the time about Clume's being in hot water and trying desperately to raise money to meet some suddenly called notes. Evidently Clume had won the battle, for the *Express* was still his; but his expression, as he looked at Wendell, told me that he retained some very unpleasant memories.

Amid a final volley of hand-clapping, Wendell dropped back into his chair. Clume turned to me, and I saw that the twinkle had returned to his eyes.

"*Sic semper tyrannis*," he said. "They get away with anything."

I hastily cancelled my contribution to the Wendell ovation and occupied my hands with lighting a cigarette. Clume chuckled.

"You'd better go ahead and applaud," he said. "I think your city editor has his eye on you."

"I'm not worried," I said pointedly, deciding at that very moment that I'd like to work for Clume. "I've got a better job lined up."

"Well, perhaps," he replied. "I suppose I could use a young red-headed Irishman. Whenever you're unemployed, let me hear from you."

 **CHAPTER 2**

ABOUT TWO MONTHS after I went to work for the *Express*, I stumbled on the biggest news story of the year. I went to the office of the district attorney one Friday morning in connection with a current case that promised to develop some interesting political angles. Breezing into the outer office, I saluted Miss Fleming with a smile that should have melted ice. But Miss Fleming had experienced that smile many times before, and it slanted off her like sunlight from a glacier.

"Mr. Cook is busy," she said, glancing at me over the top of the switchboard.

I tossed my hat and topcoat to one of the leather chairs along the wall.

"Of course," I said. "That's what he gets paid for. And as a reporter I get paid to find out what he's busy about."

"Then I'm afraid you won't get paid today," she returned. "He'll be in conference for some time."

"How about Mr. Jackson?"

"He's in conference with Mr. Cook."

"Miss Fleming," I said gently, "that's what you told me yesterday morning. Are those fellows trying to break the conference record? Now if you'll just give him a buzz and tell him —"

I stopped, noting that Miss Fleming was looking past me toward the door.

"Did you want something?" she inquired.

Turning, I saw a middle-aged woman standing near the door to the corridor. At Miss Fleming's words, she walked slowly to the desk, hesitantly, as if an invisible presence were pushing her forward against her will.

She said, "I want to see the district attorney."

Miss Fleming had become a machine, incapable of noting the nuances of tone and timbre of voice of those who endlessly made the same request. But I sensed a quality of desperation about this short, plump woman. I dropped into a chair and picked up a magazine.

"The district attorney is busy just now," Miss Fleming said.

"How long must I wait?" the woman asked.

"I couldn't say exactly. He's in conference, and I doubt whether he'll be able to see anyone today. You might try again at about four-thirty this afternoon."

The woman stood a moment, opening and closing the clasp of her handbag. Then she turned to the door, took a step or two, and swung around again to face Miss Fleming.

"I have to see him right away!" she said, and her desperation was so manifest that Miss Fleming looked interested. "I — I can't wait until this afternoon. By this afternoon I may — I may change my mind! You better tell him to see me. He'll want to see me."

"What do you want to see him about?"

"I can't tell you that," the woman returned. "It's a private matter."

She opened her purse and fumbled inside with gloved fingers. Withdrawing a card, she handed it to Miss Fleming.

"Here. Take him this. And tell him it's important — very important."

Miss Fleming looked at the card, hesitated, and then reluctantly reached for the telephone, inserting a plug into the small switchboard.

"Mrs. Oliver Embry is out here and wants to see you, Mr. Cook. She says it's very important. . . . No, she doesn't want to say. . . . All right, I'll try."

She spoke to the visitor. "Can't you give us some idea about the nature of your business? Mr. Cook says —"

"Then tell him it's about the man who was murdered on Walker Street last Monday evening," Mrs. Embry answered helplessly, looking as if she were about to turn and run from the room.

Miss Fleming repeated the message into the telephone, said, "All right, I'll get them," and hung up.

Mrs. Embry asked, "Well?"

"Mr. Cook doesn't recall the case you mentioned. He wants to see the reports on it from the police department. He'll see you, though, in just a few minutes. What's the name of the man who was killed?"

"I don't know."

Miss Fleming again had the receiver to her ear and was about to insert a plug in the board.

"You don't know?"

Mrs. Embry shook her head. "It wasn't anybody I know."

"Monday evening on Walker Street?"

"On the corner of Walker and Blair Avenue."

Miss Fleming inserted the plug and spoke into the telephone. Mrs. Embry, at Miss Fleming's suggestion, seated herself in the chair next to mine. I was apparently absorbed in the magazine.

Miss Fleming tried to catch my eye and, failing in that, spoke sharply, "There's no use waiting around, Mr. Reed. Mr. Cook won't see you today."

I laid aside the magazine and rose, picking up my hat and coat.

"Maybe I'll have better luck tomorrow," I said. "Will you try to get me an appointment? It's that beer tax evasion story I'm after."

"Yes, I know. I'll see what I can do."

I left the Criminal Courts Building and crossed Market Street to the police station. I found Captain Bruce in his office in the detective bureau.

"Hello, Captain. Can you spare me a few minutes?"

"Come on in, Red," the captain replied heartily. "What are you doing around here? Did they put you back on the old beat?"

"Nothing like that. I just dropped in to get a little information — about the man who was murdered last Monday night on the corner of Walker Street and Blair Avenue."

Captain Bruce looked at me searchingly.

"You know we just sent up the record of that case to the d. a.'s office?"

"Yes. I was there when Miss Fleming telephoned."

"What did Cook want the record for?"

"There's a woman up there who seems to know something about the case. What's it all about? Who got killed, and how, and why?"

"Critchfield got the story. Didn't you run it Tuesday?"

"How do I know? I never read the police news. It always reminds me of my humble beginnings. What happened?"

"Nothing much. At about six o'clock Monday evening a woman phoned in that a man had been shot near her house. Peterkin and Kelly investigated. They found this dead man lying on the sidewalk with two bullets in him; nothing on him for identification. In his pants pocket were four one-dollar bills and ninety cents in change; so the motive wasn't robbery, unless the stick-up shot and then ran away without cleaning him."

"Who was he?"

"We haven't found out. His fingerprints aren't on file either here or in Washington. Plainly he's a vag, most likely from out of town: ragged clothing; several days' growth of beard; filthy. Looks like he was riding the blinds and empty coal cars; coal dust in his hair and all over him."

"Where's he now? In the morgue?"

The captain nodded. "A lot of people have looked at him, but nobody's claimed him. He doesn't fit any description in the missing persons bureau. Maybe the woman you saw in the d.a.'s office will—"

"She doesn't know him. I heard her say so."

The captain frowned and pulled at his lower lip.

"Then what could she know about the case?"

"That's what I'd like to know," I said. "Cook is listening to it now, but I'll never learn anything about it from him if he can help it. He has a grudge against my managing editor and he's thumbs down on anybody connected with the *Express*. He forgets that we were practically buddies when I was doing police for the *Times*."

Captain Bruce smiled. "Serves you right for leaving a respectable paper like the *Times* and going to work for that muckraking stinksheet. That guy you're working for is screwy. Everybody knows that Asaph Clume is screwy."

That got my goat. I felt the color breaking over my face.

"If he's screwy," I said, "it's a pity we haven't more screwy people in the world. The better I know him, the more sure I am that he's a great man."

When I left the Captain's office, I went down the hall to the press room. Larry Critchfield was there; and I called him out into the hall and asked him what he knew about the Walker Street killing. I couldn't see where it amounted to much, but my curiosity was aroused. It was very possible that Captain Bruce had left out a few details which Larry, who had covered the story for the *Express*, might be able to supply.

"I went out with Peterkin and Kelly," Larry told me. "Two radio cops got there before we did. They were there within five minutes after the woman telephoned that a man had been shot near her house. The fellow who was killed was a bum, and there wasn't anything on him to identify him. He was shot twice with a .32 automatic. When the ambulance took him away, Kelly and Peterkin went to talk to the woman who had telephoned; and I listened in. She was so nervous and hysterical it was hard to get anything out of her. As a matter of fact, she didn't know very much. She heard a couple of shots, ran to the side window, and saw a man lying on the sidewalk."

"What time was it?" I put in.

"A little after six; just getting dark. But the big arc light over the intersection was on, and her house is on the corner. She could see the body plainly enough from any side window."

"That was all she knew: just heard the shots and then saw the body?"

"That's all."

"Who else was in that house?"

"Nobody else. Her husband and her daughter came home while we were questioning her. And, boy, you ought to see that daughter! I've dreamed about her every night since."

"That's swell," I said. "When you dream about her tonight, give her my love. Was there anyone else around there who heard the shots, or saw anything?"

"Not a soul."

"What about the people in the other houses?"

"There aren't any other houses. You know where Walker Street is. It's out in the Oak Hill section. Blair Avenue is a long block north of Oak Hill Boulevard. Along Walker Street there are only three or four houses, and they're closer to the Boulevard. Then there's nothing but vacant lots until you get to the Embry house on the corner of Walker and Blair."

"Embry?" I asked. "Is that the name of the woman who telephoned?"

"Something like that. Why are you interested in the case? They haven't identified the dead man, have they?"

"Not yet," I said. I lowered my voice. "Keep this under your hat. Mrs. Embry is upstairs now talking to the d. a. She came to tell him something important in connection with the case."

"But she said she didn't know anything about it!"

"Either she lied," I said, "or she learned something since then."

He shrugged. "Personally, I think she's nuts. I know it makes a woman nervous when a guy is plugged near her house; but this Mrs. Embry was in a state of collapse. You'd have thought the murderer had taken a shot at her first."

"Maybe he did."

He stared at me. "What do you mean by that?"

"I mean that we don't know what happened. Maybe Mrs. Embry didn't act as you'd expect her to act under the circumstances because the circumstances weren't what you thought they were."

He scorned the notion. "They were exactly what I told you."

"Well, maybe," I said. "It probably doesn't matter one way or another, so far as we're concerned."

That was really how I felt about it; but after years of chasing crime news, my instinct reacted to the old stimulus. I was like old John Farley who, until his retirement on pension, was a patrolman of the traffic division. He had been off the force for two years, but he was still wandering around town putting tickets on illegally parked cars. My new duties were those of political commentator. Asaph Clume let me do a daily column called "Round-Up," which was intended to be controversial. I was making a lot of enemies and having a grand time generally. My immediate concern was the stinko connected with evasions of the state beer tax and the possible implication of certain individuals in the department of finance and taxation.

I found myself crossing Market Street again toward the Criminal

Courts Building. I took the stairs to the second floor; and when I reached the upper corridor, I saw Captain Bruce get out of the elevator and hurry into the district attorney's reception room. He strode past Miss Fleming and opened the door to Cook's private office, disappearing within.

I had a hunch that he had been summoned in connection with the mysterious developments in the case of the murdered tramp, and I wondered whether Mrs. Embry was still in the d. a.'s office. I hung around the corridor for about fifteen minutes. Then Cook, Jackson, the assistant district attorney, and Captain Bruce came out of the office and stood in a solemn group near the door to the corridor. I joined them. They looked at me as if I were a fly in their soup.

"Mr. Cook," I said, "I've been trying to see you for three days. How about giving me five minutes?"

"I'm very busy, Reed," he replied, "and it would be five minutes wasted. I'm not ready for a statement about the tax cases. Early next week I'll have a press conference. I'll let you know."

"How about the woman you just interviewed? Is she still in your office?"

I may have imagined it, but it seemed to me that my question made him extremely uncomfortable. He suddenly changed his crisp, businesslike manner to one of friendly confidence.

"Oh, that!" he said lightly. "Nothing to it. She thought she might be able to identify a body. Her brother's been missing for a week. I sent her to the morgue to have a look."

I knew he was lying, but I pretended to be satisfied with his story. I turned to Captain Bruce.

"When you identify him, let us know, will you?"

"Sure, sure," the captain returned expansively. "Critchfield will get it."

I moved away, leaving them to stare after me in heavy silence.

CHAPTER 3

I HAD WORK to do on my column, so I returned to my desk at the office and tried to concentrate on my notes. I was in a surly mood. For the first time since I had gone to work for the *Express*, I was dissatisfied with my job.

I left my typewriter, with its fresh sheet of paper still innocent of political controversy, and consulted the city directory. There were three Embrys at the Walker Street address. Jane, Mrs. Oliver, was a housewife. She was forty-four years old. Oliver, forty-nine, was an accountant employed by the Wendell Arms Company. Margaret, twenty-one, was a secretary employed by the same company. Both father and daughter worked at the powder plant. They had come home together, Larry had told me, on the evening of the murder, arriving while the detectives were questioning Mrs. Embry.

That left me exactly where I had started. I was closing the directory when Asaph Clume came out of his office and caught sight of me.

"Say, Rufus, where's your column?" he called.

Guiltily I glanced at the clock that was on the wall above his head. It was five minutes to twelve. I always wrote my column in the morning and took it to Clume personally before noon for his approval. I went over to him, deciding that as long as I had to explain my tardiness, I might as well get a load off my mind at the same time.

"I haven't written a word of it," I said. "I've been trying to figure out something, and the time slipped by before I realized it."

"It will do that," he replied solemnly. "What are you trying to figure out? Come in and tell me about it."

I followed him into his office. He seated himself in his leather chair, and I perched myself on the arm of another chair on the other side of his desk.

I told him what was on my mind.

When I finished, he said, "As I see it, the most interesting point is the attitude of the police department. If the victim had been wearing a dress suit and the bullets had penetrated a pleated shirt, he'd have been identified within twenty-four hours."

"Bruce said there is absolutely nothing to work on," I replied.

"Nonsense! He meant that it may be a lot of trouble, and a tramp isn't worth it."

"I know I'm acting like a nut," I said apologetically. "Critchfield turned in a ten-line story on it, and we ran it Tuesday. That's probably all it's worth. But somehow or other it hasn't let me alone since I walked in on it this morning. I guess it's just one of my hunches."

"Remarkably reliable, though equivocal sources of information," he said. "Hunches, I mean. By all means, play your hunches, if you're fortunate enough to get any; but as a general rule, finish your column first."

I took that the way it was intended.

"Hell!" I exploded, losing my temper. "The damned column isn't my whole job, is it? Or am I to pass up what may turn out to be a good story just because it doesn't happen to fit into the column? If that's what you want, Mr. Clume, just say so and —"

"Indeed, no," he said placidly. "Curiosity is second nature with a good reporter. He mustn't try to be selective about news values. That's what editors are for. But since you are taking my remarks as a reprimand, let me justify myself. It would have been more productive to have forgotten the column while you solved the mystery or to have forgotten the mystery while you wrote your column."

"Unfortunately," I returned bitingly, "everyone hasn't your ability to concentrate."

"I appreciate the difficulties, Rufus. I'm not entirely blameless myself. When I was a young man, I decided to get married. But somehow I could never harness thought and action to the same young lady. As a consequence, I'm still a bachelor." He sighed. "Now run along and write the column, and when you've finished it, find out what the woman told the district attorney. Since Cook won't tell you, suppose you find out from the woman herself? If you can't draw water from the faucet, it's best to go to the well."

"Or drink a glass of beer," I grumbled, making for the door.

"Not if you want the water for a bath," he said as I went out.

Nobody ever got the last word with Clume.

When I went back to my desk, I found a letter that had come in the noon post. It was from a taxpayer so completely in accord with some of my columnar observations that he was moved to write at such length his welcome letter filled four-fifths of my column and saved me several hours of joyless labor. At ten minutes to one my chore was finished, and I let Jimmy Grant, the office boy, take the manuscript to Clume.

After lunch I took my coupé from the parking lot and headed for Mrs. Embry's house. Walker Street was the Western terminus of the Oak Hill bus line. There the Number 5 buses unloaded the last of their passengers, made a U-turn on Oak Hill Boulevard, and began the return trip downtown. Not many passengers traveled as far west as Walker Street, for the Oak Hill section was relatively new and, as Larry Critchfield had told me, contained more vacant lots than residences.

Mrs. Embry's was the fourth house north of the boulevard. It stood on the corner at the beginning of the second block, a square, two-and-a-half story house of whitewashed brick. I rang the door-bell several times before I heard footsteps within. Mrs. Embry came to the door, but she did not open it. It was equipped with one of those small hinged windows at eye-level, like the speak-easies used in the old days; and she swung it back and looked out at me. I couldn't see much more of her than her eyes, which were red and swollen.

"Are you Mrs. Oliver Embry?" I asked.

"What do you want?"

Her voice sounded as if I had interrupted a good cry.

"I'm from the *Express*," I said.

"The express?" she repeated. "You have a package for me?"

I was tempted to say "yes" in order to get my foot in the door. Something told me that this woman wasn't going to talk for publication without persuasion of one sort or another. But of course it wouldn't do to antagonize her.

"The *Evening Express*," I replied. "I'd like very much to talk to you about —"

"Oh! The newspaper!" she interrupted, and there was positive horror in her voice. The peephole window slammed shut.

"That's that!" I thought, getting back into my car. "If the faucet won't work, try the well; and if the well is dry, go jump in the lake!"

I drove back to Oak Hill Boulevard and started downtown, slouched gloomily behind the wheel. There was no use in trying to figure out a way to make Mrs. Embry pour out her burdened heart to me; her refusal to talk could not have been more definite. With Mrs. Embry and the district attorney's office dedicated to secrecy, I might as well forget the matter.

I reached that decision and Decatur Avenue at the same moment; but while I was waiting for the lights to change, I got an idea. I made a right turn and drove south on Decatur where, three miles out, was the powder plant. I knew I was drawing to an inside straight; and that even if I made it, the pot wouldn't amount to any-thing; but it was better to try it than to have Clume remind me that I had overlooked a bet.

The Wendell Arms Company covered a lot of territory, sur-rounded by a high galvanized wire fence and overhung by a pall of smoke that had not yet been noticed by our smoke commissioner.

My press card got me past the watchman at the gate, who told me that Oliver Embry was in the auditor's office on the second floor of the administration building. In the large room was row after row of oak desks at which sat men and women operating typewriters and comptometers. The place sounded like a field of crickets on a summer's night. I asked a young woman at a front desk where I could find Oliver Embry, and she told me that she would get him for me. She went into one of the small offices at the rear of the room, returning with a tall, thin, round-shouldered man who would have been perfectly cast as Bob Cratchet in Dickens' *Christmas Carol.*

He appeared to be surprised that I was someone he had never seen before, and there was uneasiness, too, in his pale blue eyes.

"You want to see me?" he asked in an uncertain voice. "I'm Mr. Embry."

"I won't keep you long," I said. "Can we go out there in the corridor?"

The corridor was quiet and deserted.

"I was just talking with your wife, Mr. Embry, and she told me that I should come out to see you. She said you would tell me whatever I wanted to know about that shooting last Monday evening."

His prominent Adam's apple rose above his collar line and dropped back. He moistened his lips, one with the other.

"Who are you?" he asked.

I foresaw trouble ahead but I had to rely on my deceptive opening.

"I'm from the *Evening Express.* I just want to clear up a few points about that shooting. Do you know who the murdered man was?"

It was plain to see that he was badly frightened. His hands were clasped tightly in front of him, and they were white with the pressure.

"I don't know anything about that. I wasn't even at home when it happened. My daughter and I came home later. What little my wife knows about it, she told the police. We don't know any more than that."

"I'd like to believe you, Mr. Embry," I said, "but your statement doesn't jibe with certain facts. If your wife doesn't know anything new about it, why did she call on the district attorney this morning to tell him something of great importance about the case?"

He looked as if he were going to faint. His hands fell apart, his face grew waxy, and he recoiled a few steps as from a blow.

I regarded him with astonishment. Was it possible that I had brought him news? His reaction indicated that it was news and of a calamitous nature. Plainly, I had him groggy, and I quickly followed up my advantage before his head cleared.

"Your wife was too upset to talk to me. She said you'd tell me the whole story. Of course, I don't mean the story she told the district attorney. That's public property now. But why did she keep it secret so long?"

I was working the old trick, pretending to know more than I knew. It might have been successful if this wasn't my Jonah day.

He was about to speak when a girl appeared in the doorway, inspected us with a swift glance, and then hurried toward us, saying, "Dad! What's the matter?"

So this was Margaret Embry, the girl Larry Critchfield was dreaming about. I could hardly blame him for reviving her image even in so intangible a form. With pale blond hair, too soft and full of ringlets to have been the product of a "permanent," deep blue eyes fringed with long, dark lashes, a complexion that could only be the fond hope of an ambitious schoolgirl, and a small, trim figure that was not too much here and just enough there, she was beautiful enough to recur in the dreams of a hard-boiled Hollywood casting director.

Oliver Embry turned his stricken face to her and said brokenly, "Peggy, she — this man says —" He stopped, and then the words tumbled out. "Mother went to see the district attorney!"

She was silent a moment, but I could see that the information hit her almost as hard as it had hit her father. Her arms fell to her sides, her shoulders slumped with their weight. Then she gave a small shrug of despair and helplessness.

"I thought she would," she said hollowly. "I should have stayed at home with her."

He shook his head dazedly, incredulously.

"Only this morning she promised me —"

"I know. Well, it's done now; and there's nothing we can do about it — nothing," she added bitterly, "except look for other jobs." She looked up at me as if suddenly aware of my presence. "Are you from the district attorney's office?"

"He's a reporter," her father answered. "He got the story from the district attorney and then went out to see Mother. She told him he'd better come here and —"

"A reporter?" she cut in. She seemed to see me in a new light, to sense that they were being tricked. "You say you talked to my mother?"

"Yes," I said. "I was at your house at half-past one."

"What did Mother tell you?"

"She didn't tell me anything," I replied, trying not to show how uncomfortable I felt. "I spoke to her only through that little window in the front door."

That was to convince her that I had been out there.

"Your mother appeared to have been crying. She said she was too upset to talk to me, and that I'd better come here and talk with Mr. Embry."

She kept her eyes fixed on mine. They were hard, shrewd, and, for the good of my purpose, entirely too intelligent.

"It's strange that she'd send you here," she said coldly, "when she knew that we knew nothing about her visit to the district attorney. What paper are you from?"

I took out my press card and showed it to her.

"Oh, yes — Rufus Reed. You write that column in the *Express*. You say the district attorney gave you the story?"

"I was in his office when your mother called this morning," I replied, taking my card from her.

"You were present when my mother —"

"I was in the outer office when she asked to see him."

"The outer office. I see. And as soon as she left, the district attorney told you what she said to him. Then what do you want to find out from us?"

I knew I was getting the worst of it, but I had to see it through.

"Well, there are certain details that —"

"I'm sure there are," she interrupted with heavy sarcasm. "I don't like to accuse you of lying, Mr. Reed, but I can't believe that the district attorney would immediately give out this story to the papers without a thorough investigation. Nor that my mother would send you out here."

She turned to her father. "We'd better be getting back to work, Dad."

She took his arm and led him away. I watched them until they disappeared through the office door. The shrewd vixen! I thought. If she hadn't butted in, her father would have told me everything I wanted to know. She was beautiful, all right, and maybe I'd dream of her. But if I did, you wouldn't want to frame it for a valentine!

CHAPTER 4

"I'M SURPRISED TO see you looking so gloomy," Asaph Clume said to me as I flung myself into the chair on the other side of his desk, "since you have just discovered the columnist's priceless secret, letting an obliging public do the work. I was wondering how long it would take you to discover the means of ease and indolence without the sacrifice of your pay-check."

"Ease and indolence, my eye!" I said. "I've been working this afternoon — and how!"

"You'll get over that," he said. "At the beginning the columnist supports his column; then the contributors support the column; and the column supports the columnist. Some years ago I hired a very successful columnist who had been working for another paper. He was with us for almost six months before I found out that he couldn't write a word of English. That man had a following!"

"Well," I said, "this man had better get a following because I'm hot on the trail of something that promises to keep me too busy for anything else."

I told him what had happened, leaving out nothing. While I was relating the details of my encounter with Margaret Embry, he lifted a hand to stroke his long nose and, I suspected, to conceal his amusement. When I finished, he took his hand away; and his face wore its usual expression of solemnity.

"Rufus," he said, "let me give you some helpful advice. Work your deceptive tricks on men, but never try them on women. If you had to fight a duel with a professional fencer, you'd be wise to choose pistols. Deception is women's natural weapon, and no man can beat them at using it." He paused and added solicitously, "Rufus, you seem to be nervous. Light a cigarette."

"A cigarette won't help me," I said. "I'd like to know what you make of this Embry case. What did that girl mean by saying that she and her father would have to look for other jobs?"

"Offhand, I'd say that she believed they'd lose their present ones. I wouldn't attempt to guess why."

"The whole affair is crazy," I said. "What has the murder of an unidentified tramp got to do with the jobs of a secretary and an accountant at the powder plant? Even if Mrs. Embry herself did the shooting —"

He stopped me with an out-turned palm.

"I suggested that we wouldn't attempt to guess. Let's wait a few days and see what might develop. Something — whatever it is — has started to move. There's no use in trying to follow it until we know in what direction it's going. I have an idea about how we may find out, but the time isn't ripe for trying it."

The door opened, and Larry Critchfield looked in.

"Can I come in?"

"Certainly, Larry," Clume said. "We're playing riddles in here."

"Then I'm just the man for your party," Larry returned. "I've got a few riddles myself." He looked at me. "It's about that case you were talking to me about this morning, Red. Do you remember? The tramp who —"

"I have a vague memory of it," I cut in. "What about it?"

"There's something queer going on, all right," he said. "That woman you said was in the district attorney's office this morning came back again this afternoon. I ought to say she was brought back because she arrived with Captain Bruce in his own car. It was about two o'clock, and I was standing on Market Street when I saw Bruce's car drive up to the side door of the Criminal Courts Building. When they got out of the car, I recognized the woman as Mrs. Embry. They went in through the side door, so I beat it around to the front entrance and went up to the second floor. Bruce took the woman into Cook's office. I hung around out in the corridor. After about an hour, the woman came out alone, and she was a worse wreck than when I saw her that night at her house — the night of the murder, I mean. I couldn't see any good in following her, so I thought I'd wait for Bruce to come out. He came out about fifteen minutes later with Cook and another man who must have been in there the whole time. And guess who that man was? You couldn't guess in a million years."

"Then we can't spare the time," said Clume. "Who was it?"

"Wendell!" said Larry. "Thomas Wendell!"

I looked at Clume, who had been relaxed in his chair, and noticed the slight stiffening of his body and the quick lift of his head.

When I started to speak, he said, "Just a moment!" in a voice that held a new note. For a while he sat staring at the desktop. Then he turned to Larry and asked, "Anything else?"

Larry said, "They came out of the door that leads from Cook's private office directly into the corridor. I was waiting near the stairway where I could see them without being seen. Wendell shook hands with Bruce and Cook; and I heard Cook say, 'I'm sorry about this unfortunate affair, Mr. Wendell. We'll investigate this woman and find out what's behind it. If she has some criminal purpose, I'll take the necessary steps. If she's mentally unbalanced, she ought to be put away. I hope I won't have to bother you any further.' They were walking toward the elevator where they'd be able to see me, so I beat it."

Clume said, "Rufus, your hunch seems to have been a good one. The sensitiveness of your antennæ is a valuable asset."

"Thanks," I said, "but what are we going to do next?"

"Not very much. I don't want you to attempt to speak to anyone involved in this affair. Don't let the district attorney or the police know that we're at all interested. That goes for you, too, Larry."

Larry said eagerly, "I'll just keep my eyes and ears open, Mr. Clume."

"Of course, that is their normal condition during waking hours. Rufus, beginning next Monday afternoon, telephone the powder plant daily at three o'clock and ask to speak with Miss Margaret Embry."

"But you just said —"

"I don't want you to speak with her. While she's being called to the phone, hang up."

"I see what you're after," I said. "But what's the idea?"

"Rufus," Clume said wearily, "one of the reasons why I never married was to avoid the necessity of giving reasons for what I want to do or have done. You'll be informed in good time. Meanwhile, will you please leave me alone? I have some heavy thinking to do."

 **CHAPTER 5**

AT THREE O'CLOCK on Monday afternoon, I telephoned the powder plant and was connected with the auditor's office where a woman's voice informed me that Margaret Embry was no longer employed there. I took the news to Clume who, for the first time since Friday, permitted me to mention the case.

"So the young lady's fears were justified," he said. "It's not surprising. Wendell has always demanded what he calls loyalty from his employees. He has made loyalty a form of worship, with disloyalty an unpardonable sin. The creed serves many useful purposes, especially at election time when it is an act of loyalty to vote for the candidates that Wendell wants in office. The Embrys, it appears, have been guilty of disloyalty."

"In what way?"

"That remains to be seen. We'll have to find out from the young lady."

"Not on your life!" I said firmly. "I'm not going out there and have that little window slammed in my face."

"By no means, Rufus. Instead, we'll have the young lady call on us here. Read this. I'm running it this evening."

He handed me a slip of paper on which he had written:

WANTED: Young woman secretary, some experience. Good salary. Apply in person Tuesday morning between 10 and 11, Editorial Rooms. EVENING EXPRESS.

"It won't work," I said. "That girl is too smart to fall for it. She'll see through it the minute she reads it."

"Of course she will," he agreed. "We're making her an offer, and I believe she'll accept it. Arrange to be in the office at ten tomorrow and when Miss Embry calls, bring her in here."

Girls began to stream into the city room before nine o'clock, and it was my unpleasant duty to meet them near the head of the steps and tell them that the position was filled. I must have turned back several dozen applicants by ten o'clock and I decided that braining Asaph Clume would be justifiable homicide if Margaret Embry did not show up.

But promptly at ten she appeared, mounting the rickety narrow stairs and paying no attention to the girls who were going down and trying to save her a useless climb. When I saw her, I called Jimmy Grant and gave him a sign to tack on the wall at the foot of the steps. It looked like the job was filled, all right.

She waited while I repeated my sad story to several girls.

When I was free she came over to me, unsmiling, and said, "I got your message, Mr. Reed."

She must have thought that one up on the way to town. She was just the type to prepare herself thoroughly for an ordeal, even to framing a greeting that would show me that she hadn't been fooled.

I took her to Clume's office and went in with her, for Clume had asked me to be present during the interview. He got to his feet as we entered, and I saw that he wasn't going to put on an act of an employer interviewing a job-seeker.

"Good morning, Miss Embry," he said pleasantly, without waiting for a needless introduction. "I appreciate your calling. Won't you sit down?"

She was first to speak after everyone was seated.

"We may as well understand each other right from the beginning," she said, meeting Clume's eyes levelly. "I knew what your ad meant as soon as I saw it. But I'm taking your offer literally, Mr. Clume. I need a job now more than I've ever needed one, and I'm ready to make a trade for one."

"I like your frankness," Clume replied, "and, if you'll permit me to manifest the same trait, I like you. When Mr. Reed told me of his meeting with you the other day, I was sure that you were a most unusual young woman."

Color touched her pale cheeks. She looked at me but spoke to Clume.

"I'm afraid I was awfully uncivil to Mr. Reed. I was angry because he tried to work a trick on us. And of course he brought news that upset me terribly."

"Forget it," I said. "I got what was coming to me for leading with my right."

She stared at me.

Clume said, "Mr. Reed means that by his tactlessness he laid himself open to your indignation. Not knowing you, he underestimated your intelligence. I'm sure that he wouldn't make that mistake again."

I smiled at her. "Not while I'm conscious."

An answering smile flickered on her lips, then died away as she turned again to Clume.

"I suppose you'd like to get down to business," he said. "I can offer you a secretarial position at a salary of forty dollars a week. As salaries go today, that is somewhat above the average."

"It's fifteen dollars more than I was getting. Would it be permanent?"

"My dear young lady," answered Clume, "that is a question for the oracle. Permanence is a condition set by the optimist who reckons without his host."

I saw a chance for getting even.

"Mr. Clume means that the job is yours until one of you drops dead, or the paper goes into bankruptcy."

Clume looked at me.

"Thank you for clarifying the matter, Rufus. But you should have stipulated your own possible unexpected termination since Miss Embry would be your secretary."

I opened my eyes. "Mine?"

"That is what I plan. I notice that your mail has grown very heavy since yesterday, and it's probable that most of the literate people of Rutherford County will soon be writing to you. An intelligent secretary who will read the contributions and select the best ones for the column will give you greater leisure in which to cultivate your mind."

He turned to the girl, who was taking it in and, it seemed to me, enjoying it.

"You will recall, Miss Embry, that in my advertisement I specified that I wanted a young woman with some experience. The word 'some' was used advisedly. Any experience wouldn't do. It must be a specific experience relating to the murder of a tramp a week ago last evening."

"I know," she said. "That's what I meant when I said I was willing to trade for a job."

"Good."

"If I tell you my story, I'll expect you to keep your promise and give me that job."

"Of course. That's agreed."

"But in all fairness to you, I think I ought to warn you that the story will be without value to you. You won't want to publish it, Mr. Clume."

"That will be for me to decide. Tell me."

"I'll tell you as briefly as I can," she said, "but I don't want to leave out anything. You know about the murder of that tramp, and that it was my mother who called the police. Mother told the police the truth, but not the whole truth. And in one particular, it wasn't exactly true. She said she was in the kitchen when she heard two shots, then looked out of the living room window, and saw the man lying on the sidewalk. This is what really happened: She was upstairs in her bedroom that evening. My father and I always came home from work together, usually at a little past six, and Mother was in the habit of standing at the upstairs window watching for us. From the side corner window she could see quite a way up Walter Street toward Oak Hill Boulevard where we got off the bus.

"That Monday evening she was watching for us as usual. It was just getting dark. There's a bus that reaches Walker Street at about five after six. Dad and I missed that one at Decatur Street and took the one that comes along ten minutes later. At approximately seven or eight minutes past six, Mother saw a man coming down Walker Street toward our house from the boulevard. I mean, in that direction. When he got to Blair Avenue, he crossed it and stood a moment on the corner, practically underneath the window where Mother was standing, as if he were undecided whether to continue down Walker Street or to turn west on Blair. It was too dark for Mother to see him clearly; but she could see that he looked like a tramp and she was uneasy. Since we moved out there last year, she's been a little nervous about staying alone in such a quiet neighborhood.

"Anyway, while the man was standing there on the corner, an

automobile came up Walker Street from the direction of the boulevard. It was going pretty fast, but not exactly speeding. It passed
Blair Avenue and the tramp standing there and went on up Walker
past our house. The tramp seemed to make up his mind where to go
and started walking west on Blair. He had taken a few steps and
was directly under the window, when the automobile appeared again
at the corner, now going slowly and facing the boulevard. Then it
stopped, and a man called from the car, 'Hey, there!' or something
like that. The tramp turned around, and a man got out of the car
and walked toward him. He walked right up to him, and when he
was about a foot away, he suddenly pulled his right hand out of his
overcoat pocket and fired two shots in quick succession. The tramp
staggered and fell forward on his face. Then the other man knelt
beside the body for a moment as if to determine whether the man
was dead.

"It had grown dark rapidly in the past five or ten minutes, and this
action wasn't very distinct. But just as the man rose to his feet from
beside the body, the street light suddenly went on. There's a big
arc light over the intersection, and it's so bright that Mother and
Dad often complain it shines into their bedroom all night. The light
took the murderer by surprise; and he made a dash for his car, got
in, and drove away down Walker Street toward the boulevard. But
Mother says that she got a perfectly clear view of the murderer,
even of his face. She says that it was Mr. Wendell!"

The girl paused, and Clume opened his eyes slowly.

"I guessed as much," he said. "Had your Mother ever seen Wendell, or only his photograph?"

"She's seen him a number of times. She and Dad go to the affairs
given by different organizations of employees at the plant, and Mr.
Wendell always appears to give a talk. She says she'd know him
anywhere. She's been seeing him ever since 1919 when he took
charge of everything after his uncle died. Dad was employed at the
plant for twenty-six years. He got his first job from Mr. Arnold
Wendell, and he's never worked for any other company. You can
imagine what getting fired now means to him!"

Clume said, "'Now tell me the rest of your story, and then I may
want to ask a few questions."

"Well, Dad and I got home at about fifteen or twenty past six.
We found Mother being questioned by two detectives and a reporter.
She was in a dreadful nervous condition; and as soon as the men
went away, we took her upstairs and put her to bed. We couldn't
understand her going to pieces like that until she told us what she

hadn't told the police. When she told us that it was Mr. Wendell who had shot the tramp, well, we didn't know what to think. Dad tried to show her that the thing was preposterous; that Mr. Wendell wouldn't drive past a tramp on the street, come back and stop his car, get out, and shoot the man dead. It was simply impossible. But Mother was absolutely convinced. She said she had to believe the evidence of her own eyes, and she had seen Mr. Wendell's face clearly and had recognized his stiff-legged walk. There wasn't the slightest doubt in her mind that Mr. Wendell had murdered the tramp.

"For the next few days we were all in a terrible state. Mother's guilty knowledge — or what she called her guilty knowledge — was preying on her mind. She thought she had done wrong not to tell the police everything and that it was her duty to go to the police or the district attorney and tell what she knew."

Clume said, "You and your father opposed that action. You knew that if she brought that accusation against Wendell, you'd both lose your jobs at the plant."

"Yes, we knew that. But that isn't really why we didn't want her to tell. We thought she was — mistaken."

"Just what do you mean by that? Do you mean that it's a case of mistaken identity? That she saw a man who resembles Thomas Wendell?"

"That could be. Or it could have been someone purposely trying to look like him, even imitating the way he walks."

"Hmmmmmmmm."

"But the most likely explanation is that Mother is simply mistaken. It was a terrible experience for a woman alone in the house, standing there at the window in an unlighted room and looking out into the half-darkness. You must remember that the street light went on only an instant before the man ran to his car and drove away. In that moment of great excitement Mother may have fancied a resemblance to Mr. Wendell."

"It's quite possible. But your mother is so positive that she can't admit the possibility?"

"She says she's as sure it was Mr. Wendell as she is that there's a God in Heaven. Lately I've had reason to doubt that, too," she added with a trace of bitterness.

Clume shook his head reprovingly.

"Tell me, has your mother good eyesight?" he asked.

"Perfect. She reads the finest print and does the most delicate embroidery without glasses."

"She has normal vision in faint illumination? She hasn't some degree of night-blindness, has she?"

"I don't think so. Her eyes are good."

"Can she describe the car that drove up? Did she get the license number?"

"No. The district attorney questioned her about that Friday morning. She doesn't remember the car at all. She says it was a closed car, but she can't remember whether it was a coupé or a sedan. She said she didn't really look at the car; she was watching the men."

"Unfortunate, but perfectly natural. I suppose the district attorney makes much of your mother's inability to describe the car."

"Yes, he does. Under pressure, Mother finally said she thought the car must have been a sedan. They put that in her signed statement. No doubt, Mr. Wendell owns large cars, but he usually drives a Lincoln coupé."

"I suppose your mother told you everything that occurred at the district attorney's office when she went down there voluntarily Friday morning and when they brought her back again in the afternoon?"

"Yes. They took her in to face Mr. Wendell in the afternoon."

"I know that. And she stuck to her story?"

"Except for the statement about the sedan. She went back to her original statement that she didn't remember the car. Otherwise they haven't been able to shake her story at any point."

"They've tried to since Friday?"

"Oh, God," she moaned. She lifted her hands and for a moment pressed her fingers against her eyes. "They've come to the house again and again. It seems there's always someone there, torturing Mother. One detective has been there five or six times, a stout, red-faced man —"

"Captain Bruce?" I said.

"Yes, Captain Bruce. He's been out a few times alone, and once the district attorney was with him, and yesterday afternoon, both of them came back with a doctor. The doctor took Mother into a room alone and talked with her for over an hour. I guess he was a psychiatrist. Later he talked to me and Dad about her. He questioned me about her general behavior in her relationships with the family and other people, especially within the past few years. He talked a long time with Dad alone."

Clume said, "I hope you were careful in your replies."

"Of course I was. I admitted that I thought she must be mistaken in her story about Mr. Wendell, but I assured him that she was perfectly all right mentally, never unusually nervous, or gloomy, or anything like that. She sold herself on that idea and she won't let go."

"Have you seen or spoken to Mr. Wendell?"

"No. He doesn't stay out at the plant. His office is in the Wendell Building. On Saturday we found the pink slips in our pay envelopes. When I went to say goodbye to the man I was secretary to, he said he didn't know why I was being fired; that he had simply received orders to let me go."

"Miss Embry," Clume said, "aside from the fact that you have earned a job when you sorely need one, you'll never regret having taken me into your confidence. This is a time when a feller needs a friend, and I'm going to be your friend. You and I have a common enemy, and it's well that we stand together. It's common knowledge that I don't like Thomas Wendell and never did. Many people think that it's a personal matter, but it isn't. I don't so much dislike the man as what he stands for. I have no objection to his wealth. As Mr. Reed would phrase it, I'm pretty well heeled myself. I object to the way he uses his wealth. He ought to be an employer, but he's a feudal lord. He ought to be a prominent citizen, but he's an absolute monarch in a make-believe democracy. He's not at all like his uncle Arnold, whom I knew very well and thought highly of. He's an upstart; and like all upstarts, the sudden acquisition of wealth and position went to his head. A man who is born to wealth, or who acquires it slowly and laboriously through his own efforts, usually recognizes it as a means to service. The man who gets it suddenly and without effort sees it only as a source of power, and he uses it accordingly. I'd have more use for Thomas Wendell if he were an out-and-out tyrant. He's all the more dangerous because he's a hypocrite."

She heard him with amazement, looking at him with round wide eyes.

"But, Mr. Clume! Everybody thinks so highly of him! He's so — so philanthropic and —"

"That's the form of his hypocrisy. His civic benefactions are bribes. Whenever he wants certain men elected to office, or certain laws enacted, and he isn't sure that he can control enough votes through the power of employment, financial indebtedness, and first mortgages, he gives the city or county a park, a library, a monument, or some other expensive bauble. Then he tells a grateful public how to vote. As a consequence, we have the most corrupt and vicious state, county, and city government in the country. It's a government of, for, and by Thomas Wendell. That's why I don't like him."

Her incredulous amazement was enlightening. This girl, who a little while ago had doubted God, found it difficult to doubt Thomas Wendell.

Clume went on, "That's all that will be required of you today, Miss Embry. Go home and rest and report for work tomorrow morning. Your salary will start this morning."

I took her out; and when I returned to the office, Clume was in the same position as when I left.

"What do you think of it now, Mr. Clume?"

He looked at me as if I had taken him only partly from his thoughts.

"Rufus, that girl is exceptionally attractive," he said. "Be careful."

 **CHAPTER 6**

EARLY THE FOLLOWING morning, Clume called me into his office. He asked me whether the Embry girl had come in, and I told him that I had put her to work reading the six letters addressed to me.

"Beyond that," I added, "I can't think of anything for her to do. I'm afraid I got you into making a bad bargain, Mr. Clume. We can't use an extra stenographer around here, much less a secretary."

"Don't worry about it, Rufus. We'll manage to find enough work for her to keep her satisfied. Why do you think I made a bad bargain? Isn't her story interesting?"

"Not to the extent of forty bucks a week. Now that I've heard it, I'm willing to forget it. It's a case of 'that's that,' so far as I'm concerned."

"Then you conclude that it's incredible?"

"And impossible," I said, "if that makes it any stronger."

"Incredible, yes," he returned, "but not impossible."

I stared at him.

"You don't intend to publish the story, do you?"

"I haven't made up my mind about that. I'd like to, of course. It's a story that deserves publication, but the *Times* or *Star-Herald* wouldn't touch it. If anyone besides Wendell were involved, it would already have been given to the papers. By withholding publication I'm conspiring with the very forces I usually fight." He paused and closed his eyes. "I can see the banner head: THOMAS WENDELL ACCUSED OF MURDER. Then: WOMAN IN AFFIDAVIT CHARGES MILLIONAIRE MANUFACTURER WITH FATAL SHOOTING — Rufus, how would you like to write that story?"

"It's OK with me," I said; "but who'll pick up the pieces?"

"There's no risk. We would be reporting actual news. Mrs. Embry made her affidavit, and it's in the district attorney's office. I believe, though, that we'll wait awhile. I've promised to help the Embrys, and I can protect them better if I'm armed with a club. So long as I know the story but haven't published it, I'll be in a better position to trade with Cook."

"He'll railroad Mrs. Embry to the state asylum," I said. "She can save herself by retracting her story; and if she doesn't, he's probably justified."

"What if her story is true?"

"Then I'm the Prince of Pilsen," I said, "and you're my cousin Sidney."

"An interesting example of mistaken identity," he returned; "which is just what I have in mind. Somehow, I don't believe that Mrs. Embry is insane. If she were a victim of delusion, her family would have noticed previous signs. And, apparently, she didn't concoct the story for the purpose of getting Wendell in trouble. As a means of revenge, the accusation is too far-fetched. Furthermore, if either Mr. or Mrs. Embry, or both of them, felt any enmity against Wendell, the daughter would have shared it to some degree. I eliminated that possibility by telling the girl what I thought of Wendell. I wanted to note her reaction. Don't fidget, Rufus. I'm using you for target practice, so that when I go gunning I'll be able to shoot straight. You are a man of action and few words; I'm a man of many words and few lost motions. That's because you are twenty-five, and I am sixty. Unlike you, I can't feel that I have forty or fifty years in which to rectify any mistakes I may make."

"I wasn't exactly fidgeting," I said. "I just can't disagree with anyone and sit still at the same time."

"This strange affair isn't meaningless, Rufus. The tramp was murdered, and someone murdered him. Mrs. Embry accuses Wendell, and there's some reason why she did so. I've dismissed two possible reasons, insanity and revenge. Three possibilities remain: She actually saw Thomas Wendell, or someone resembling him, or someone deliberately impersonating him."

"In that case," I said, "it must have been someone impersonating him. There may be someone who looks a lot like him, but it isn't likely that he'd have a stiff right leg."

"Exactly! But if someone were deliberately impersonating him, would he have been confounded by the sudden illumination of the street light and made a dash for his car? He'd have welcomed the street light as an aid to his plan."

He paused to let that sink in; then he continued, "Only one possibility remains, and that is made tenuous only by our unwillingness to believe it. I won't dismiss it until I'm at least as justified as I am in dismissing the others."

"I can give you a hundred reasons offhand," I said. "But one will be enough. No one cimmits a murder without a motive."

"Well?"

"Can you tell me why Thomas Wendell would meet a tramp on the street and murder him?"

"No, I can't; but that doesn't preclude the possibility. A conclusion must be based on known facts. Since we don't know any facts, we can't reach any conclusion. But before we get busy ascertaining facts, we'd better try to look ahead. The district attorney will do everything in his power to force a retraction from Mrs. Embry. That would release him from an unpleasant and uncomfortable situation. Like you, he disbelieves the story on general principles, and he isn't interested in determining whether it's true or false. But I am. I don't want her to retract if it's true."

"You needn't worry about that," I said. "Margaret Embry told me this morning that her mother was determined to stick to her story no matter what they do to her."

"Excellent! We must see to it that they don't do too much." He pushed back his chair and got to his feet. "Let's go and have a talk with Cook."

The district attorney made us warm reception room chairs for twenty minutes, but he finally let us enter his office. He ignored me and curtly greeted Clume, who did not wait to be invited to sit down but settled himself in a high-backed chair near the desk. I took a chair behind him, over near the window. This was his party.

"I've come across a news story of unusual interest," Clume said. "I know you agree with me as to its interest because you've tried to keep it quiet. I'm referring to Mrs. Embry's affidavit charging Thomas Wendell with murder."

I expected to see the district attorney fall out of his chair, but he didn't bat an eye.

"I thought you must have heard of it. I've been told that Mrs. Embry's daughter is now in your employ. What about it?"

"That's what I've come to ask you, Mr. Cook. Before I publish the story, I want to give you the opportunity of telling the public what you plan to do about it. You can't very well follow your inclination to ignore it. A man has been murdered, and another man has been accused of the crime. I find it necessary to appropriate your question. What about it?"

Cook was silent for a moment. He sat straight in his chair, regarding Clume with stony, calculative eyes.

Then he said: "What do you think I'm doing about it? If I were to make a public statement, I'd say that being a man of judgment and reason, I completely discredit the woman's story. Mr. Wendell is the last man in the world any reasonable person would suspect of such a crime. If there were overwhelming evidence against him, I'd be reluctant to believe it. And as it happens, there's no evidence whatsoever. I'm making, and will continue to make, every effort to get at the bottom of the absurd accusation. If I find that there's any criminal involvement, such as malicious gossip or blackmail, I'll take the necessary steps. But in my opinion, it is merely the product of a diseased mind. In that event, we'll see that the woman receives the proper medical attention." He paused. "That's my statement. Do you want it typed and signed?"

Without waiting for a reply, he opened a desk drawer and took out a typewritten paper, reached for a pen, and signed his name at the bottom.

"Here, Mr. Clume," he said, handing the paper across the desk "I have this copy of the statement I gave to the *Star-Herald* this morning. I'm sorry you won't be the first to use it; the *Star-Herald* will carry it in its noon edition."

I left my chair and stood where I could look at Clume. If he felt as shocked as I did, he didn't show it. He read the paper casually folded it, and put it in his pocket.

"It doesn't do you justice," he said to Cook. "While it's fairly conclusive regarding the accuser and, at least by implication, whitewashes the accused, it completely ignores the third member of the infernal triangle, the murdered man. You seem to have forgotten him in your eagerness to absolve Wendell."

Cook shrugged. "There's nothing much to say about him until we establish his identity, and the police are working on that. Unfortunately there's nothing at all to work on, but they're doing the best they can. You may be interested to learn that Mr. Wendell, through the *Star-Herald*, is offering a reward of five thousand dollars to the person who can identify the murdered man."

Clume was taking it on the chin, and I felt sorry for him. He was feebly pawing at an opponent who was beating him to every punch, and I wanted to toss in the sponge and call it quits. Clume was game, anyway. Apparently unmoved, he sat among the wreckage of his pretty plans.

CHAPTER 7

BY THE TIME we left the d. a.'s office, the noon edition of the *Star-Herald* was on the streets. The headline was as large and black as Clume could have desired. It screamed: PLOT AGAINST THOMAS WENDELL SIFTED.

Under the caption, "Do you know this man?" were two photographs of the murdered tramp taken, of course, in death. In one, his face was covered with a dark stubble of beard; in the other, he was shaven. In a box with boldfaced type was Wendell's offer of five thousand dollars reward. I folded my paper and tucked it under my arm. I had seen all I wanted to see.

"That just about lets him out, doesn't it?" I said.

"We forced his hand, Rufus."

"Yes," I agreed dryly; "and he laid down a straight flush. We lost the scoop, the story, and the club we were going to use to save Mrs. Embry from the asylum. I think we'd better call it a session and try to sleep off the headache."

Clume shook his head. "Not just yet. Wendell has smoke-screened the issue, but nothing has happened to throw any light on the real mystery. He's a brilliant strategist, Rufus, who believes that attack is the best defense. His action doesn't incriminate him, but neither does it clear him. Guilty or innocent, he would have acted just this way."

I said, "I can take it if you can. What do we do next?"

"We'll get your car and drive out to see Mrs. Embry," he replied. "It's about time we're having a talk with her."

When we reached Walker Street, a bus was making a U-turn on Oak Hill Boulevard. Clume watched it.

"Is this the end of the bus line?" he asked.

"Sure," I said. "It's Walker Street. This is where we turn. The Embrys live a block down."

"Why of course!" he murmured, as if to himself. "That explains it!"

I turned the corner. "Explains what?"

"How the tramp happened to be where he was when he was shot. Didn't you tell me that he had some money in his pocket?"

"Four-ninety," I said. "Four one-dollar bills and ninety cents in change." I stopped the car in front of the Embry house. "Does that explain anything?"

"I think so." He opened the car door. "Let's get an impression of Mrs. Embry."

It was Mr. Embry who came to the front door, inspecting us through that confounded peephole. But when Clume gave his name, he opened the door and invited us in. He wore his alpaca office coat, and on his feet were a pair of old leather slippers. He looked thinner, paler, and more thoroughly woe-begone than when I saw him at the powder plant.

"Excuse the way I look," he said penitently. "I — I'm just staying around the house these days." His throat was husky, and he cleared it with his hand over his mouth. "Mr. Clume, I'd like to say how grateful I am to you for employing my daughter. Peggy told us how kind you were to her — to all of us, for that matter."

Clume said, "You needn't thank me, Mr. Embry. I don't pretend to have been prompted by pure generosity. I'm glad, of course, that I'm able to help you while helping myself."

A door opened at the rear of the hall, and Mrs. Embry came out. I was surprised to note the change that had come over her. Despite the troubles that were piling up and the menace of definite peril, she had been able to buck up. She was pale, with the skin too tightly drawn across her face, but she showed none of the hysterical panic and desperation of a week ago. She came forward, unsmiling and yet not without friendliness, and offered her hand to Clume.

"I heard Oliver thanking you for helping us," she said. "With everybody down on us, it's comforting to know that — Did you decide to publish it? Is that why you've come?"

"It wasn't left for me to decide," Clume replied. "Wendell's paper, the *Star-Herald,* just came out with it."

He took the paper from his pocket and handed it to her. While she and her husband read it, Clume and I removed our topcoats and laid them across a chair. I watched Mrs. Embry's face as she read. She compressed her full lips into a thin line, and the jaw muscles bulged in her cheeks. She skimmed over the article and after half a minute she folded the paper.

"I'll read it later," she said. "I knew what they'd say. *I'm* the criminal! *I'm* the dangerous woman!" Her voice dropped. "It — it's hard to believe."

Clume said gently, "Shall we sit down and talk it over?"

She took us into the living room at the left and we all sat down. Mrs. Embry looked at Clume.

"Do you know what they're going to do with me, Mr. Clume? If they can't send me to jail, they're going to put me in an asylum."

Clume nodded. "I know their intentions."

"They say I can save myself by changing my story. Is that logical? If they think I'm crazy, how can they let me at liberty just because I say I lied? I said that to the doctor, that alienist they brought out here, and he looked as if my statement convinced him that I was crazy." Her hands were closed into fists on her lap. "I'm not going to change my story. I'm not going to say I lied when I didn't. If I'm to be punished for doing my duty as a good citizen, then I'll have to stand it, somehow."

"You have courage," Clume said, "and it will help you through this trouble. All of this might have been foreseen before —"

"I did foresee it. That's why I waited from Monday night until Friday morning before going to the district attorney. I knew that if my own husband and daughter wouldn't believe me —" She broke off, hopelessly. "But what's the use talking? It was just my misfortune to have been standing at that window. I saw a man killed and I recognized the man who killed him. I have nothing against Thomas Wendell. I don't know him well, of course, but I always liked him. Why should I want to get him in trouble, even if I could? My husband worked for him, and for his uncle before him, for twenty-seven years. My daughter worked for him for the past two years. This house and everything in it, the clothes on our backs — everything we have comes indirectly from Mr. Wendell. But what has all that to do with it? I saw him kill a man and I simply had to tell what I saw. Wasn't that my duty, Mr. Clume?"

"Unquestionably. Not many people recognize their duty, and very few would sacrifice themselves to do it."

Oliver Embry, who was sitting forward on the edge of the divan and rubbing his thighs with his palms, spoke timidly.

"And sometimes it just isn't worth it. A person must consider the consequences." He put his fingers against his lips and cleared his throat. "I told her what would happen to us. I told her they wouldn't believe her and would think she's crazy."

Mrs. Embry looked at him as if she would like to hit him. Then she turned to Clume.

"Not even my own family stands by me. I suppose that when the time comes, they'll be among the first to swear away my sanity."

Clume, his face long and solemn, looked steadily at Oliver Embry.

"Let me ask you a point-blank question, Mr. Embry. Do you believe that your wife is mentally unsound?"

Embry was aghast. "Why, of course not! I only think she made a terrible mistake."

"But since she is so positive that she saw Thomas Wendell, why do you insist that she made a mistake?"

"Mr. Clume, on the very face of it —"

"Never mind the face of it," Clume interrupted impatiently. "The face of the earth appears flat. If you don't doubt her sanity, how do you account for her actions in this affair?"

"I can't account for them."

"Then let me give you some advice, Mr. Embry. Keep your opinions strictly to yourself. Your wife has a battle before her and she needs all the support she can get. Your faith in her would greatly strengthen her defense. Conversely, your lack of faith must be one of the strongest points against her."

Embry's face wore a stricken look.

He said pathetically, "I intend to stand by her. I want to get a good lawyer to defend her. I — I'll spend my last penny to help her."

I looked at Mrs. Embry and saw that her eyes were swollen with tears.

"In nearly twenty-five years," she said throatily, "this is the first thing that's ever seriously come between us. I guess I can hardly blame him. I guess I can hardly blame anybody. What I saw — well, it's not easy to believe. But I saw it. I saw it so plainly! At first I doubted my own eyes. I told myself that it couldn't have happened as I saw it. But deep down inside of me, Mr. Clume, I knew that there was no mistake. When that light went on, there he was, standing just below me. The bedroom window is directly over this one, and they were right out there on the sidewalk."

After a pause Clume said, "That picture you carry in your mind. I want you to close your eyes and put it before you. The tramp has been shot and has fallen to the sidewalk. What is the other man doing?"

She had her hand over her eyes.

"He stoops over the man and turns him over."

"Was the tramp lying on his face?"

"Yes, and he turns him over on his back."

"What then?"

"He drops to one knee beside him. I suppose he's trying to make sure he's dead."

"Is he putting an ear against the tramp's chest?"

"No, he isn't bending over that far." She took her hand away from her eyes. "It was pretty dark then. That was before the street light went on."

"Please close your eyes again. Don't try to remember. Just recall the picture and tell me exactly what you see. The man is kneeling beside the body. What is he doing?"

"It's too dark," she said despairingly, her eyes still covered. "I can't see what he's doing."

Clume tossed his head a little, impatiently or, perhaps, in disappointment.

"Well, what happens now?"

"He gets up. And now the light goes on!"

"It's Wendell?"

"Oh, yes! It's Wendell!" She moaned the words.

"Look at him well. Has he anything in his hands?"

"The revolver's in his hand. The right hand. I see it."

"Has he anything else?"

"I don't see anything else. Now he's putting the revolver into his overcoat pocket, while he looks at the lower window and then up at the bedroom window. I see him so clearly! Then he turns and runs stiff-legged to his car —"

"Now look well! Can't you see that car?"

"Yes! Now I can! *Now* I can! It's a big coupé. It's long and shiny under the light — and it's green!" She dropped her hand and stared at Clume. "I saw it then, and I was never before able to remember it."

"Let me ask you, Mrs. Embry," Clume said gently, "if the police or the district attorney said anything to you about the car Wendell drives? Did anyone tell you he drives a Lincoln coupé?"

"Yes, they did. Mr. Cook said so. At first I said I couldn't remember the car. Then they — they pounded on me until I said I thought it was a sedan. When I said that, the district attorney told me that Mr. Wendell never drives a sedan but a Lincoln coupé."

"A *green* Lincoln coupe?"

"I don't think he mentioned any color. I don't remember. But that wouldn't make any difference. I just saw that car in the picture, exactly as I must have seen it that evening. It was a light-green coupé."

Clume gave his chair the backward hitch that signaled his impending departure. He took his heavy gold watch from his pocket, snapped open the cover, and snapped it shut again. Then he rose, shaking down his trouser-legs, and we all got to our feet.

When he and I were back in my car and headed toward the boulevard, I said, "That woman has almost convinced me. I'm on the verge of believing her damn fool story."

"It's nearly half-past one, Rufus," he replied. "Let's stop at the first restaurant. My mind works better when it isn't visualizing food."

CHAPTER 8

IN THE DISPATCHER'S office at the barn of the Fairmont Bus Company, we learned that William Kress, Number 721, was conductor of the Oak Hill bus that reached Walker Street at about six o'clock in the evening. He was on the second shift during October and reported for work at a quarter to three to take the three o'clock bus out of the barn.

It lacked five minutes of that time, so Clume and I stood near the door and waited. After a while our informant gave us a sign, and we returned to his window in the cage. A middle-aged man, stout and red-faced, stood there.

"These gentlemen want to see you," said the man behind the cage. "This is Mr. Clume, the publisher of the *Express*." He added jovially, "Maybe you'll get a write-up, Bill."

The conductor shook hands with us.

"Can you spare a few minutes?" Clume asked. "I'd like to have a talk with you."

Kress took us to a bus in the barn, and we sat down on the cross seats at the rear.

"This will be mine today," he said, "so we'll hold it down until my driver shows up. What do you want to talk to me about?"

"How good is your memory, Mr. Kress?" inquired Clume.

"It's pretty good."

Clume said, "I want to see if you can recall a passenger. The time is a week ago last Monday, October 9th. The bus is the number 5 that reaches the end of the line at Walker Street at about 6 P.M. Somewhere along the route a man got on the bus. He stayed on until the bus turned at Walker Street, where he got off. He paid his fare with a five dollar bill. You gave him four ones and ninety cents in change."

Clume paused. The conductor pushed back his peaked cap and scratched his head.

"That's a large order. It's not so unusual for a man to hand me a five-spot."

"This man," put in Clume, "didn't look like the kind to pay his fare with a five dollar bill. He was a tramp. His clothes were ragged and dirty; he needed a shave and a haircut."

A flash of memory illuminated Kress's face.

"By God, I do remember! It was a tramp, like you say. When he handed me that five spot, I kind of gave him the once-over, wondering where he had lifted it. I took a good look at the bill, too, but it was good. He stuck with the bus till we got to the end of the line. He was the last one to leave. Most passengers get off before we get to Walker Street. When we made the stop on the north side of Oak Hill Boulvard, before making the turn back east, he was still sitting tight. I called in that it was the end of the line, so he got up and swung off. I can't really remember what day that was. I just remember the dirty tramp with a five spot."

"Can you remember where he got on?"

Kress puckered his lips, squinted his eyes, and thought hard.

"Let me see now. Maybe I can. He got on somewhere downtown. It was somewhere on Broadway below Eighteenth where we turn north to Oak Hill. Oh, sure; it was further downtown, between Seventh and Twelfth, I'd say. We'd made a stop for passengers; and just as we started away, this man ran out of a store on the corner and jumped us."

"One more question," said Clume. "Did he have any money besides that five dollar bill?"

"That's all I saw. He pulled it out of his pants pocket. It wasn't on a roll, or I think I'd have called a cop just on general principles."

The bus driver approached and swung aboard, and Clume and I took our leave.

When we left the barn and made our way to my car, I said, "Your guess was pretty good, Mr. Clume. Now we know how the tramp happened to be where he was when he was shot. But the answer makes things all the muddier. The man who shot him — whether it was Wendell or someone else — couldn't have been laying for him because he couldn't have know where he was going. The tramp himself didn't know. He got off at Walker Street only because that's as far as the bus would take him. I suppose he walked north on Walker because he happened to be on the north side of Oak Hill when he got off — But wait a minute! Do you think his murderer followed the bus until he got off?"

"A reasonable assumption, Rufus."

"There isn't much choice," I said. "It's either that, or we must believe the murderer just happened to pass by and had a sudden whim to get out and kill him."

We reached my car and got in. I sat behind the wheel, thoughtfully swinging my chain of keys on a finger.

"Mrs. Embry said the car came down Walker Street from the boulevard. It was following the tramp, of course. But why did it pass him at the corner and then come back?"

"For two reasons, I should say," Clume answered. "First, in order to give the driver an opportunity to see whether the coast was clear. Second, so that he could turn the car around to be facing the boulevard for a quick get-away."

I thought it over and decided that the explanation satisfied me. But the trouble with this case was that the more I found out about it, the more confusing it became. Before the interview with Mrs. Embry, I was willing to believe that she was mentally unbalanced. I didn't believe that now. Nevertheless, her story remained incredible, and what we had learned about the tramp prior to his murder did nothing to lessen its incredibility.

"We've got that tramp traced back to Broadway, somewhere between Seventh and Twelfth," I said aloud. "If we could go on from there, we could find out who he is and collect Wendell's five grand."

"We'll let someone else collect the reward. The offer and the man's picture will be reprinted in papers all over the country. The claimants are going to be as thick as flies. It will have to be a matter of first come, first served. We'll know the man's identity before the week is out."

"And then we'll be sure that we've been wasting our time," I said, starting the motor. "Do we go back to the office?"

"You will," he replied, "and see what you can do about tomorrow's column. Drop me off at the Mercantile Trust Building on the way."

When I entered the city room, I saw that the *Star-Herald's* bomb had practically wrecked the place; and a fog of gloom hung over the ruins.

I walked to my desk across the room. Margaret Embry sat there, doing nothing and looking as if she had been doing it for a long time.

To give her something to do and make her feel that her employment wasn't an act of charity, I dictated my column to her, though I wasn't used to dictation and I could have pounded it out faster on the typewriter. I had just finished it when Clume came in and called both of us to his office.

He said that he had retained Daniel Howard, the criminal lawyer, in behalf of Mrs. Embry.

"Now we'll let the district attorney make the next move," he added. "He'll probably let matters rest until the dead man is identified. Then he'll renew his efforts to force a retraction. When he does, your mother is to get in touch immediately with Mr. Howard. His office is in the Mercantile Trust Building and his telephone number is State 4323. Make a note of that number and have it handy at home so that there will be no delay when it's needed. If the district attorney sends for your mother or goes to the house to see her, she must refuse to leave the house or to answer any questions until she has contacted Mr. Howard. Is that clear, Miss Embry?"

She nodded.

"I'll leave it to you to instruct your mother. Tell her not to worry about the consequences. Whatever Cook threatens to do is sheer bluff. Criminal action is out of the question; she took her story directly to the district attorney, making no attempt to see or write to Wendell and without telling her story to friends, or neighbors, or to the newspapers. Commitment proceedings before a sanity commission wouldn't get very far. Your mother is obviously sane." He paused. "Those are our battle plans. Let's hope that there will be a battle."

Startled, she exclaimed: "You hope — !"

"This morning, your mother thought that she remembered the murderer's automobile. She described it as a large green coupé. I just found out that the car Wendell drives is an apple-green Lincoln coupé!"

"She didn't remember that," Margaret said. "The district attorney told her."

"Just what did he tell her? That's what I want to find out. Did he say that Wendell's car is a Lincoln coupé or a *green* Lincoln coupé?"

I asked, "How can you find that out?"

He turned to me.

"That conversation took place in the afternoon when Captain Bruce and Wendell were present. That was when Mrs. Embry dictated the formal statement that she signed. A stenographer was present, of course. Everything that was said at the hearing was taken down verbatim. There's only one way we can get a look at that record. Mrs. Embry's attorney is privileged to study the case from the beginning. He has no standing, however, if no action is taken against his client. Let's hope that some action will be taken."

CHAPTER 9

ON SATURDAY the *Star-Herald* scored its second beat of the week. Here are some informative excerpts from the story:

The combined efforts of the police department and the STAR-HERALD to establish the identity of the victim of a mysterious shooting which took place in the fashionable Oak Hill District on Monday evening, October 9, reached a successful conclusion late last night when the dead man was identified as Vincent Creel, 25, unemployed machinist, of Toledo, O.

Identification was made by a brother, Henry Creel, 21, also from the Ohio City. . . .

Claiming the reward offered by the STAR-HERALD, Henry Creel appeared at police headquarters late last night. After viewing the body at the County Morgue, he accompanied Chief of Detectives Captain Richard Bruce, to the home of District Attorney Ben Cook where, after presenting photographs, snapshots, and other satisfactory sources of identification, he was subjected to a lengthy questioning. He told the following story:

"My brother and I left Toledo early in August and took to the road. We had both been out of work since April and could find no employment. We were restless and decided to move on.

"We got to Fairmont about 5 o'clock Monday afternoon. We made our way from the railroad yards to the downtown section. We separated on the corner of Ninth and Broadway, agreeing to meet at the same spot at 8 P.M.

"I left my brother at a quarter past five and walked up Broadway. That was the last time I saw him alive. I passed a restaurant on

Tenth Street south of Broadway (Kohler's) and went around to the alley door. The cook bargained to give me a square meal for helping in the kitchen. I peeled spuds and washed dishes there until nearly eight o'clock and earned a good feed and four bits besides.

"Then I went back to Ninth and Broadway to meet my brother as we had planned. I waited until 9 o'clock, but he didn't show up. A cop questioned me and told me to beat it out of town or I'd get locked up.

"So I went back to the yards and found a freight headed east. I figured that my brother had been scared out of town earlier and I thought I'd find him in Toledo.

"I rode the rods of a passenger train a good part of the way and reached Toledo Tuesday night. The next day I got my job back at the factory and I've been working there ever since. Last Thursday I read about the murder in the paper and saw my brother's picture and the offer of the reward. I borrowed money from friends and took the first train to Fairmont."

A police check-up verified Creel's story in every particular. Asked if he or his brother knew Thomas Wendell, he said:

"Neither of us ever saw or heard of Mr. Wendell. Until Monday afternoon we had never been in Fairmont in our lives and had never even been in this state. We know nobody here." ...

Reading that, I thought: Wendell got his five thousand dollars' worth.

I dropped in to see Captain Bruce Monday afternoon and found that his amiable mood had returned. No longer troubled by the delicate features of the case, he was perfectly willing to discuss it.

"Nobody in his right senses would have believed that woman's story," he said; "but the identification of the body puts Wendell entirely in the clear. Vincent Creel never laid eyes on Wendell, and Wendell never saw Creel. Why, the man wasn't in town an hour before he was shot. We checked up on that. We found a brakeman who saw Creel and his brother get off the freight."

"But the fact remains that somebody plugged him," I said; "and the circumstances that clear Wendell seem to clear everyone else. He didn't know anybody in town, and nobody knew him. Then who killed him, and why?"

"I think he was mistaken for somebody else. No other theory is possible."

"Do you think Mrs. Embry is crazy?" I asked.

"Damned if I know. Considering her story and the way she sticks to it, she probably is. But otherwise she talks and looks sane enough. If she isn't crazy, she'll come clean and admit she made up the whole story. The d. a. will see to that."

That was what I wanted to know. If Cook intended to drop the matter, Clume would have run an editorial that would stir him to action. Clume was determined to know exactly what had been said to Mrs. Embry about Wendell's automobile.

Taking leave of Bruce, I walked to Ninth and Broadway, following up a clue that was as thin as a strand of cobweb. The thirty-two-story Wendell Building covered the entire block from Ninth to Tenth Streets, with the Broadway entrance at the center of the block. On the corner of Ninth was a cigar store. The adjoining stores were a railroad ticket office and a fashionable haberdasher's, and it wasn't likely that Vincent Creel had entered them. He must have dashed out of the cigar store to catch the bus.

I went in, bought a package of cigarettes, and waited around until several customers made their purchases and left. Then I introduced myself to the young man behind the counter and gave him some idea about what I was after.

"I'm not talking," he said. "I don't want to get messed up in that case. Look what's happening to the woman who —"

"That's different," I cut in. "You're not talking for publication, and I'll never mention your name. I just want to know if you saw that tramp in here around five-thirty Monday evening."

"Well, I didn't."

"Oh, come on!" I said. "You've as much as told me that you remember him. And I happen to know that he ran out of this store to catch a bus. Be a sport and help me, won't you? What did he come in here for?"

"You promise not to write me up?"

"So help me God!" I said.

After a moment he said, "Well, I do remember him. From what the papers said, he wasn't a crook, but he certainly looked plenty tough. He came in on the double-quick, and there weren't any customers here at the time. I took one look at him and was ready to stick up my hands. But he went on past me to the back of the store and entered a telephone booth. He closed the door and the light went on, and I kept my eye on him."

"Did he use the phone?"

"No. I noticed especially that he didn't use the phone. He was in that booth back there, the last one to the right. I could see him from the waist up. He seemed to be looking at something or reading something that he held in his hands; but I couldn't see what it was."

"Maybe he was looking at the directory," I suggested.

"Maybe. There's one in every booth, hanging from a hook in the wall. He was in there at least five minutes, and meanwhile a few customers came in and went out. At a time when the store was empty, he came out of the booth and asked me if I could let him have a pencil. He had a decent way of talking, not at all tough, so I felt easier about him. I gave him a pencil, and he went back into the booth. After a while, he came out and handed me my pencil. Then he made a sudden dash for the door, almost knocking over another man just outside the doorway, and jumped on a bus."

"Did you get a look at the man he bumped into?"

"No. I watched the tramp until he got on the bus, and by that time the other man had moved away."

I said, "I'm certainly obliged to you. If I can ever do you a favor, I'll be glad to do it. Sometimes I can get a traffic ticket fixed or something like that."

"It's good to know somebody with pull," he said. "Let me tell you something else. I'm in charge here from noon until 9 P.M. At about eight o'clock that same night I saw the man that identified his brother and copped that five thousand dollar reward."

"You saw him standing out front?"

"He came in here. He bought a package of cigarettes and I gave him change for four bits. What makes me remember him is that he went back to the phone booths. He went into the first one, closed the door, and stayed a minute. Then he went into the second booth, and then into the third one. He didn't use the phone in either one. When he came out of the third booth he left the store and walked away. Isn't that queer?"

"Queer is right," I agreed.

"I didn't give it any thought until I read about the identification in the paper Saturday. He said he waited for his brother on this corner until nine o'clock, but he didn't. He went away as soon as he left the store. I figured that his brother might have left a message, and he came in to find it. Why else would he go from one booth to another?"

"Where would he leave the message?"

"That's what I was wondering. There's no hiding-place except between the pages of the directory; and the way that hangs from the hook, a paper would likely fall out. I looked at the walls of the booth, but there's nothing there except a lot of telephone numbers. Then I thought that it was written in the book somewhere. I turned every page from cover to cover and didn't find anything."

"Maybe the second man tore it out of the book," I said.

"I thought of that, too. But there isn't a page missing."

"I'd like to check up on that," I said. "Our sports editor gave me two ringside tickets to the Heeney-Randolph fight at the Hippodrome next Saturday night. They're yours if you let me borrow that directory until tomorrow."

As soon as I returned to the office, I went in to see Clume. Placing the directory on his desk, I told him what I had learned from the clerk.

"I'm sold on the message idea," I said. "And I don't see where he could have left any except in the directory. But the clerk said he looked at every page of it. Nothing written in it and no pages missing."

"Nevertheless," Clume replied, "the message is here."

I stared at him. "How do you know?"

"I can see it."

The directory, about an inch and a half thick, lay on the desk before him. It was the autumn issue, delivered during the first week of October, and it was in good condition. It was only slightly soiled and not at all dog-eared. Clume hadn't touched the book; he merely sat forward in his chair looking at it. I walked around the desk and stood behind his chair, squatting so as to see the book as he saw it. He pointed to the front-edge of the directory.

"Do you see those lines of dots, Rufus? Pencil marks."

"If that's a message," I said, "it must be in Morse code."

He shook his head. "Have you never heard of fore-edge painting? It's an old art. In my library at home I have an eighteenth-century book decorated with fore-edge painting. When the book is closed and in its normal shape, the fore-edge has a mottled appearance. When you press down the binding and smooth out the fore-edge, a painting appears, an excellent painting of a woodland scene. I've never known the principle to be applied to writing secret messages but this seems to be a sample of it. Watch!"

He turned the book around so that the front-edge faced us. With his fingers he pressed downward and backward on the cover, and as the front-edge spread, the pencil marks stretched like rubber until they took the form of printed letters:

STRUCK SOMETHING THAT LOOKS LIKE BIG MONEY DON'T HANG AROUND WILL MEET YOU AT HOME LATER VIN.

CHAPTER 10

AT SIX O'CLOCK on the following evening, I knocked on the door of a room at the second-best hotel in Toledo, Ohio. A broad-shouldered young man with sun-coarsened blond hair and tanned skin opened the door and invited me in while he shook my hand.

"You newspaper fellows never seem to get enough," he grinned. "I thought I'd seen every one of you in Toledo since I got home Sunday night. And I guess I talked to every newspaper man in Fairmont before I left there."

"Not all of them," I said. "I'm from Fairmont."

His eyes opened wide. "From Fairmont!"

"I just got in town on the four-twenty this afternoon. I got your address at the office of the *Blade* and here I am."

"Have a seat," he said. "If you came five hundred miles just to see me, you rate a drink."

He went to the bureau on which stood a quart of whisky, a bottle of ginger ale, and several tumblers. While he poured the highballs, I looked around the room. It was a large corner room with a private bath. On the bed were a number of parcels, some of them opened to reveal shirts, socks, and other apparel. The clothes he wore were new, from his necktie to his shoes. He saw me looking around.

"Nice diggings?" he said, handing me my drink. "I just moved in here when I come back from Fairmont. Maybe you think that bed don't feel swell after a few months on the road!" He sank into a chair and stretched out his legs. "No fooling; did you come from Fairmont to see me?"

"On the level," I said.

He lifted his drink and drained it, setting the empty glass on the floor.

"What's the big idea? I told everything I know. All you had to do was read the papers."

I said, "What I want to know wasn't in the papers. I happen to be wise to something that nobody else knows, not even the police. I mean that message your brother wrote on the telephone directory."

Surprise jerked him out of his lolling position. He sat up straight on the edge of his chair.

"What the hell are you talking about?" he demanded.

I didn't like the tone of his voice or the sudden belligerency that darkened his face.

I said, "Listen, we began this talk with a handshake and a drink.

47

Suppose we keep things friendly? As a matter of fact, you aren't in a position to act any other way, considering the message you forgot to tell the police about."

"I don't know nothing about a message."

I got up and put my half-empty glass on the bureau.

"In that case," I said, "there's no use wasting time. There's a message, all right; and I've got the directory in the safe in my office. Naturally I thought you knew about it. The clerk in the cigar store saw you enter the telephone booth that Monday evening. But since you don't seem to remember, I'll just let the police worry about it."

I had my hand on the doorknob before he stopped me.

"Wait a minute!" he said tensely. "I'll play along with you."

"That's better." I returned to my chair. "I know why you didn't say anything to the police. You were afraid they might hold up the reward."

He wet his lips with his tongue. "They probably would have. Believe me, they didn't hand over that certified check until they were satisfied that I'd told them evertyhing I knew. If I had told them about the message, they'd have thought I knew still more — and I don't."

"You wouldn't hold out on me, would you?" I asked with a trace of sarcasm.

He raised his right hand. "So help me God, that's the truth! If you read that message, you know as much about it as I do. Except for that, I told everything to the cops and I gave it to them straight. When I left Vin, I went to that restaurant, just like I said. I got back to Ninth and Broadway a little before eight o'clock. Vin wasn't around, so I went into the cigar store to look at the telephone books. We learned that stunt of secret writing when we were kids, and this summer we used it on the road whenever we needed to. Sometimes one of us couldn't be at the place we planned to meet at a certain time, so we'd leave a message in the store nearest the place we were to meet. I didn't know he'd left a mssage in that cigar store. I just looked, and there it was."

I said: "Now come clean. What did the message mean?"

"I don't know." There was a pleading note in his voice, begging me to believe him. "You read it. Can't you see he wasn't writing about anything I knew?"

"He said he struck something that looked like big money."

He nodded. "That don't make sense to me. I left him at about five-fifteen. At six o'clock he was dead. That leaves about forty-five minutes for everything to happen."

"You can figure it closer than that," I said. "He was on a bus for twenty-five minutes. That leaves twenty minutes for him to strike something that looked like big money. He was in the telephone booth at least five minutes. That leaves fifteen minutes. He couldn't have got far from that corner."

He flung up his hands in a helpless gesture. "It's got me. He certainly didn't have time to get mixed up with any mob that would bump him off."

"Nor with anyone else, it seems to me," I added. "That's why I have a hunch that he had some plans even before he got to Fairmont."

"You're dead wrong," he told me earnestly. "We never planned to go to Fairmont. The train just took us there, and we were hungry so we got off. It wasn't until we were pulling into the freight yards that we knew what town we were in. All we were after was something to eat, and then we were going to leave town. We wanted to get back here as soon as we could."

"I'm trying hard to believe you," I said; "but you'll have to admit it looks phony. In the space of ten or fifteen minutes he struck something that looked like big money. I've been batting around Fairmont for a good many years and I haven't struck anything that looked like medium-sized money. Maybe he suddenly decided to rob a bank."

He took me seriously.

"Vin wouldn't do that," he said. "We met a number of guys on the road who asked us to pull jobs with them. Vin was scared to death of the police. That would have kept him straight if nothing else did."

"There's something about his message that doesn't sound straight to me," I said. "And considering what happened to him —"

"Listen," he broke in, "maybe this means something and maybe it don't. There was one kind of job that I think he would have pulled if he got the chance. A few years ago one of the fellows in the plant where we were working got something on one of the bosses. This fellow was a friend of ours, and he told us about it. It seems he was in the shop late one night, finishing some work. For some reason, he went upstairs where the offices were, and he saw a light in one of the offices. He walked right in, and there was this guy with a girl. He had the goods on 'em — see — and the boss knew it. Besides what could have happened to his big job at the factory, he was a married man. Well, from that time on, our friend had it soft. He got a foreman's job with a big boost of salary and he always had a lot of dough to spend. I guess he shook down that fellow for plenty. He still had that graft the last time we saw him."

He paused, and I asked, "What about it?"

"Well, Vin always said that the shake-down was the only kind of crooked business that paid. He said it was pretty safe, and all you were doing was making some guy pay through the nose for doing something he shouldn't have done. You can't shake down a square-shooter, can you? It has to be somebody who's getting what is coming to him."

"What about it?" I repeated. "Do you think your brother caught somebody in a compromising position on the corner of Ninth and Broadway? That was certainly high-speed blackmailing. He had fifteen minutes in which to get the goods on someone and apply the pressure of threatened exposure. All on a downtown street corner during the rush hour. And half an hour later he was murdered. You'd better try again," I said, "because my mind can't work that fast."

He sank back in his chair.

"You asked me what I thought the message meant, and I'm doing the best I can. I can't help it if it don't seem to make sense. I know how Vin's mind worked."

"Fast," I said caustically. "Like lightning."

"Listen," he said suddenly. "Maybe that sounds impossible. But what about the jack the cops found in his pocket? He had four-ninety on him, and if he spent a dime for bus fare, he had five bucks when he got on the bus. He didn't have a red cent when I left him. He managed to get hold of a five-spot within fifteen minutes, and that's more than either of us had at one time since last spring. Where did he get it?"

"That's what I traveled a thousand miles for," I said, concluding my report to Clume. "Henry Creel is on the level; I'm sure of it."

"In that case," Clume returned, "your trip wasn't wasted, as you seem to think. Although it added no startling new facts, it cleared away a number of confusing probabilities."

"It's a pleasure to work for you," I said, "because you're so easily satisfied. All I found out was that Henry Creel doesn't know anything, and that he vaguely suspects that his brother had a tendency toward blackmail. That's interesting considering he had barely fifteen minutes in which to indulge his tendency "

"Yes. Isn't it?"

"Okay," I said. "I'll turn in my expense account tomorrow. Where's Peggy?"

He lifted his brows. "Peggy?"

"Margaret Embry. I didn't see her in the city room."

"I asked her to stay at home with her mother. Shortly after you left, the district attorney got busy. He and Bruce went to the Embry home and renewed their efforts to make Mrs. Embry retract. She followed my instructions and got in touch with Daniel Howard. He went out at once and counseled her to answer no more questions. Then he called Cook's bluff, telling him either to stop bulldozing his client or to take some definite legal action. Cook didn't like that, and he got Wendell to swear out an insanity complaint. Nothing further has been done about it, but Howard managed to get the transcript of the proceedings in Cook's office that first afternoon."

He paused, and I asked eagerly, "What did he find out?"

"I read it last night. Cook told Mrs. Embry that Wendell drives a Lincoln coupé, but no mention was made of the color."

"Couldn't Mrs. Embry have learned it from some other source?"

"I don't see where. She hadn't seen Wendell for three or four months prior to this murder, and he has been driving that particular car for only three weeks. His old one was maroon. I called on Cook this morning and in the course of conversation I asked him to tell me the color of Wendell's automobile. He didn't know. I then called on Bruce, and *he* didn't know. I'm inclined to believe that I helped Mrs. Embry to remember." He took out that ponderous watch of his and looked at it. "Five-thirty, Rufus. Let's adjourn until tomorrow."

When I left his office, I heard the telephone on Jack Boley's desk ringing. The city editor wasn't there to answer, so I lifted the receiver. I heard an excited voice.

"Hello! Mr. Boley? This is Critchfield!"

I said, "This is Reed, Larry. Boley's stepped out for a minute. What's on your mind?"

He poured words into my ear, and I listened with my mouth wide open. Clume came out of his office, took one look at my face, and came over to the desk. I got through with Larry and put away the phone. It was no wonder that Larry had stuttered. When I spoke to Clume, I almost stuttered myself.

"Wendell's been murdered," I shouted, "and they've arrested Margaret Embry!"

CHAPTER 11

THOMAS WENDELL'S SUITE of offices, on the twenty-ninth floor of the Wendell Building, was neither large nor sumptuous. It was familiar to me. Like most of the reporters in the city, I had gone there occasionally for interviews. Wendell had always given interviewers a cordial welcome so long as they asked the right questions about the right things.

It was ten minutes to six when Clume and I entered the outer room. About forty minutes had passed since the discovery of Wendell's body, the reporters had come and gone, and detectives were at work in the private office. The door between the two rooms was open, and I saw Captain Bruce, Kelly, and Peterkin of the homicide squad, and Lieutenant Jordan of the bureau of identification. We put our hands in our pockets and walked in. Jordan was powdering the furniture and taking finger-print pictures. Wendell's body had been removed to an undertaker's, Bruce told us, and Peggy Embry had been taken to the police station.

"We don't know what happened," I said. "What did she have to do with it?"

"From the looks of things, she did the shooting," he replied. "Anyway, she was found in here with the body. I heard her story, but I haven't questioned her fully."

"Is the district attorney questioning her?" Clume asked.

"He's out of town. Left early this afternoon and he can't get back before late tomorrow." He paused; and when he spoke again, there was a note of respect in his voice. "I guess I owe you an apology, Mr. Clume."

"An apology?" said Clume. "What for?"

"When you told me this morning that the Wendell case wasn't finished but had only begun, I said you were talking nonsense. I didn't realize you knew something —"

"I must correct that," Clume interrupted. "When you say I 'knew something,' you imply that I'm an accessory after the fact. Let us say that my prediction was based on intuition, or even deduction, but not knowledge."

I said, "I don't understand. Did you predict Wendell's murder?"

Captain Bruce answered me.

"Mr. Clume didn't go that far. He just warned me that there'd be further developments. I thought he was talking through his hat." He looked at Clume. "Did you suspect that the Embry girl —"

Clume, mildly annoyed, interrupted again.

"Captain Bruce is probing me tactfully," he said to me. "He isn't sure whether to view me with suspicion or respect." ʼ

Lieutenant Jordan joined us.

"I'm through here, Captain. I didn't get anything but those bloody prints on the edge of the desk. I'll check up on those. I'll give you a report on the gun sometime tonight."

Bruce nodded. "I'll be in my office until late tonight. I'm going there now and question some witnesses." He turned to Clume. "Would you like to come along?"

He went to Wendell's desk and picked up the telephone.

"Hello, Grady? This is Bruce. Did you get hold of the people who work in Wendell's office? . . . All right, I'll be there in five minutes. Send someone to the Wilson Mortuary for the bullet they take from the body and turn it over to Lieutenant Jordan with the autopsy report."

He put away the telephone and said, "Let's go, fellows."

Clume said, "Can you wait a minute or two, Captain? I'd like you to show me the way this room looked when you first saw it. Where was Wendell's body?"

Bruce pointed to the floor. Midway between the outer end of the desk and the wall, the rug was stained with a drying pool of blood.

"He was lying here. He was shot once — in the throat. The bullet got him under the chin and seems to have ranged upward. We'll know its course when we get Dr. Dale's report."

"Any evidence of a struggle?" ʼ

"The chair behind the desk was overturned. Nothing else. Wendell might have knocked it over backwards if he found himself facing a gun and jumped to his feet."

Clume nodded. "Anything else you can tell me?"

"That's about all. The shot was fired at ten minutes past five. The time was established by a man who heard it as he was leaving his office. He thought it came from the street." He paused. "Those bloody fingerprints on the edge of the desk will help us. The girl had blood on her hands. She wiped it off on her handkerchief."

"I'm anxious to hear her story," Clume said. "I can't understand why she came up here, unless —"

"Come along, then. You'll hear the whole thing."

It seemed like old times to be let in on the ground floor of a police investigation. Why was Bruce suddenly so friendly? I wondered as we sat in the Captain's office, waiting for Margaret Embry to be brought in. I could account for it only by the facts that the district attorney was out of town, and Wendell was dead. Perhaps I was being unfair to Bruce, but I found myself reflecting that Fairmount's strong man was a corpse, and no one knew who would step into his shoes. In the coming struggle for succession, Clume must be reckoned with; and I supposed that Bruce considered it politic to establish friendly relations — just in case.

Margaret Embry entered the office, and behind her was Harry Thompson. Thompson seated himself at the back of the room, his stenographic notebook open on his knee.

My heart contracted when I looked at Peggy. Her attempt to be game made her more pathetic than hysterical tears. Her face was dead white, her eyes abnormally large; and though she tried to hold herself erect and walk with a firm step, her knees buckled a little as if barely able to support her. Clume got to his feet and went to her, helping her to the chair that had been placed for her.

When she was seated, he said, "Don't be frightened, Margaret. We're standing by, you see."

Now the tears welled into her eyes. She reached out and caught hold of his sleeve.

"I didn't d-d-do anything, Mr. Clume! I — didn't kill him!"

Clume patted her hand.

"Then you certainly needn't be afraid. You'll be given every opportunity to clear yourself. Isn't that right, Captain?"

Bruce said, "Absolutely!"

"Repeat your story and answer the captain's questions. *Truthfully*, Margaret!"

"Do you want me to tell everything from the beginning?"

"Yes."

"Then first I'll tell you why I happened to go to Mr. Wendell's office." Her voice was steady now. "I've been working for Mr. Clume but I felt that he really didn't have any place for me. I got a good salary but I knew that I didn't earn it. I — I felt that I was taking charity." She looked at Clume.

"Well, I made up my mind to try to find another job. Mr. Clume told me to stay at home for a few days to — to —" She broke off and looked again at Clume.

He said, "Go ahead. Tell everything."

"In order to be with my mother. So I didn't go down to work this morning, though I knew that mother didn't need me. I decided to take advantage of a day off and try to find a new job. I set out early this morning and I kept going all day. I tried one place after another from nine o'clock this morning until four-thirty this afternoon. Nobody had a job for me.

"The last place I tried was the National Investment Company. They're on the ninth floor of the Wendell Building. It was about a quarter to five when I left there. I was tired and discouraged."

"Who did you talk to there?" Bruce asked.

"A Mr. Harris. He said he had no place for me at present but he made a note of my name, address and telephone number. He'll remember me."

"All right. Go on."

"I took the elevator to the street lobby, and when I got down there, I came to a sudden decision. I made up my mind to go up and have a talk with Mr. Wendell. I didn't know him personally, but, as you know, I worked at the powder plant for several years, and my father worked there for twenty-six years. I thought that if I had a straightforward talk with him and told him how Dad and I really felt about Mother's accusation, maybe he'd understand that Dad and I weren't in any way responsible and give us back our jobs.

"Anyway, I took an express elevator to the twenty-ninth floor and went to Mr. Wendell's office. The outer office, I mean. When I asked one of the girls there if I could see Mr. Wendell, she called over a man who said he was Mr. Hammond, Mr. Wendell's secretary. He asked me what I wanted to see Mr. Wendell about, and I told him that it was a personal matter. He insisted that I state my business, so I finally told him who I was and what I wanted. He said he was quite sure that Mr. Wendell wouldn't want to see me; but if I wanted to, I could write him a letter; and then he would decide whether or not to give me an appointment.

"I didn't like Mr. Hammond. I didn't like his manner, or what he said, or the way he said it. But there wasn't anything I could do. I left the office and went down to the street lobby. I was furious with Mr. Hammond for turning me away." She stopped, frightened by her use of the word "furious." "Maybe I shouldn't have said that. But I wasn't angry with Mr. Wendell. I was just heartbroken because Mr. Hammond had spoiled my plans. I knew I couldn't accomplish anything through correspondence. I had to see Mr. Wendell personally. That was my only chance of success."

"I left the building and walked down Broadway to the corner of ninth. I kept thinking about the whole day of failure while I was waiting for the bus. Finally a Number Five came along, but instead of getting on it, I turned away and walked back to the Wendell Building. It was then about ten minutes past five.

"When I got to Mr. Wendell's office, I found the entrance door closed and locked. Everybody had left. I knew then that I was beaten and might as well give up. But just as I turned away, the other door opened and a man came out into the corridor. He came out of Mr. Wendell's private office. I thought hopefully, Mr. Wendell must still be in there! So I just stood where I was.

"The man walked to the elevators and almost immediately one stopped for him. When he was gone, I went to the second door and tapped on the glass. Nobody answered, so I tried the knob to see if the door was locked."

"Let me interrupt you there," said Bruce. "When you talked to me up in the office, you didn't tell me anything about a man."

"You didn't give me time. You told that policeman to take me away and you'd talk to me later."

"Well, all right. You say a man came out of the office just before you went in. What did he look like?"

"Well, I — I didn't get a good look at him. I didn't see his face at all. I don't think he even saw me standing there down the corridor. He came out backwards, pulling the door shut after him. His back was to me. Then he walked away to the elevators and got on one almost immediately."

"But you have *some* memory of him, haven't you? even if you didn't see his face? Was he tall, short, thin, fat? What did he look like?"

"He was about medium height and rather stout. Not real fat, but stout. His shoulders were broad. He had a queer walk — not lame exactly — well, I guess you could call it lame. Like he was lame in one leg."

"Which leg?"

"I don't remember. He walked kind of side to side."

"What else do you remember about him? How was he dressed?"

"He was shabbily dressed. He didn't wear an overcoat, and his coat didn't match his trousers. He wore a black felt hat, and it was old and shapeless. He looked almost like a — like a tramp."

"Hmmmmm — a tramp. Now that's very interesting. Well, go on with your story."

"Where was I? Oh, yes. I tried the door to see if it was locked, and it opened. At first I didn't see anyone. The office looked empty. I took a step or two inside, and then I saw — I saw Mr. Wendell lying there on the floor. He was stretched out on his back — just as you saw him — and covered with blood. I did a foolish thing then. I should have gone right out and got help. Instead of that

I knelt on the floor beside the body and tried to see if he was dead or still alive. That was how I got that blood on my hands. I saw that he was dead and I got to my feet. I stood there a moment, suddenly realizing my position, my hands covered with blood, a revolver on the floor at my feet — I was terrified. I tried to wipe the blood from my hands with my handkerchief. Just then a man passed the door which I had left open. He saw me, and then he saw the body. That's all I can tell you."

CHAPTER 12

IN THE BRIEF silence that followed, I looked at Peggy with annoyance. I thought, You little idiot! Why didn't you stick to the truth? Why did you spoil an air-tight story with that hokum about the mysterious tramp?

Of course I knew why. She was afraid that the simple truth wasn't enough; it needed adornment. That was bad enough, but her choice of adornment was worse. A tramp! A tramp with a limp! I had given her credit for too much sense to try anything so obvious. It was as transparent as clear glass.

Her story concluded, Bruce let her rest a moment.

Then he said, "You say that you went up to Wendell's office in order to plead with him to take you and your father back into the powder plant. Weren't you also going to plead with him to drop his insanity complaint against your mother?"

She shook her head. "I decided not to mention that."

"Why?"

"For two reasons. I didn't want to ask too much for fear of getting nothing. And I wasn't concerned about the complaint against mother. It wasn't important whether he withdrew it or not."

Bruce stared at her. "Where did you get the idea that an insanity complaint isn't important?"

"I was told that it was just a bluff."

Bruce shifted his position in his chair.

"Who told you that?"

Clume saved her from the embarrassment of answering that one.

"I did, Captain," he said. "It was another of my prophetic utterances."

Bruce turned back to Peggy.

"That's all for the present. You aren't under arrest, and no charge is being made against you. I'm going to let you go home."

She closed her eyes and drew a deep, quivering breath.

"But understand this," he added severely, "You must see to it that you're available at any time we want you. You're not to attempt to hide out or to leave the city. Is that clear?"

"Certainly. I'll be at home any time you want me."

"All right, then. Thompson, see that Miss Embry is permitted to leave. Take her to the door. Then bring in Roger Hammond."

When Peggy was gone, Bruce said doubtfully, "I suppose I did the right thing to let her go. Cook would probably have held her."

"Not for long," Clume returned. "Only until she could get a *habeas corpus* hearing. There's no case against that girl."

"I'm not so sure of that. Her story would ring truer if she hadn't said anything about a tramp coming out of Wendell's office. I don't mean to say that the falsehood shows she's guilty of shooting Wendell. Guilty or innocent, people will try to lie themselves out of trouble. But when you know that part of a story is a lie, you can't help feeling that it's all a lie."

Clume, slumped down in his chair, rubbed his nose.

"What makes you so sure, Captain, that a shabbily dressed man didn't come out? Someone killed Wendell. The shot was fired at ten minutes past five. In that case, it's likely that the killer would leave the office at just about the time Margaret Embry says she saw him leave."

Before Bruce could reply, Thompson reentered the office with a tall, thin, dour-faced man of about thirty-five. He verified Peggy's story about her visit to the office, though it was plain that he felt no inclination to help her. He had talked to her, he said, at about ten minutes to five.

"Why didn't you let her see Mr. Wendell?" Bruce asked.

"I didn't think it was safe," Hammond replied. "I recognized the name, of course, and I knew the trouble that Mr. Wendell had been having with that family. Besides, there was something about her appearance — well, a sort of desperation — that warned me. When I refused her request, she became abusive. She said that no twenty-dollar-a-week clerk was going to turn her away like that! As a matter of fact," he added darkly, "I'm not a clerk, and my pay is a good deal more than twenty a week. Anyway, it just shows the mood she was in. I knew then that I had judged her correctly."

"What time did you leave the office?"

"At five minutes past five. The two young ladies left at the same time."

"Was Mr. Wendell in his office when you left?"

"Yes. He told me he was staying for a while, but that it was all right for me to leave."

"Did you tell him that the Embry girl had called?"

"Yes. And he said I was right to keep her out. He didn't want to be bothered with her."

"Did Mr. Wendell say why he was staying in his office? Was he expecting anyone?"

"He didn't tell me, but I know he wasn't expecting anyone and didn't plan to stay very long. The garage had already delivered his car and had left it on Broadway in front of the building. They always left it there a little before five; and if Mr. Wendell expected to stay late, he had me phone the garage to postpone delivery. The man from the garage would park the car in front of the building, give the keys to the girl at the information desk in the lobby, and the girl would phone up to tell me that the car was there. Today she phoned at a few minutes before five."

"Was it unusual for Mr. Wendell to remain after you left?"

"On the contrary, he usually left after we did. We would lock the door of the reception office, and he would leave from his own office. I should say that he usually left about a quarter past five. As I told you, if he expected to stay much later than that, he would postpone delivery of his car."

"Did he have many callers today at his office?"

"About as usual. But no one out of the ordinary, except that girl."

"Did a shabbily dressed man ask to see him?"

"Not to my knowledge. Everyone who called on him during the past week or two was someone familiar to me."

Clume took a memo. book and pencil from his pocket and wrote. He tore the page from the book and handed it to Bruce, behind the desk. Bruce read, his brows drawn together and his lips puckered. Puzzled, he looked up at Clume.

Clume said, "Please; if you don't mind."

Bruce turned to Hammond. "Did you read Mr. Wendell's mail before he saw it?"

"Not all of it. I looked over all the mail and opened any that didn't look personal — those addressed to the Company, bills, ads, and so forth. The others I put on his desk unopened."

Bruce turned inquiringly to Clume.

Clume said, "May I ask a question or two?"

Bruce nodded.

"Did you keep any record of incoming mail?" Clume asked Hammond.

"No."

"Have you a pretty good memory?"

"I have a very good memory," he replied stiffly.

"I'm sure of it," Clume said ingratiatingly. "A good memory is characteristic of a man in your position."

"That's true," Hammond agreed, melting under the warmth of flattery. "Mr. Wendell used to say that I have a mind like a filing cabinet."

"In that case," said Clume, "I wish you'd search the mental files for a very special bit of information. I'll admit that this requires a most extraordinary memory, but by your own admission, you have it. Could you tell us what time — approximately what time — Mr. Wendell left his office on October ninth? That was two weeks ago last Monday."

Hammond looked dismayed.

"I could hardly be expected to remember that," he protested defensively.

"But let me remind you of something that sets October ninth apart from other days. On that evening a tramp was killed, and Mr. Wendell was later mistakenly or criminally accused of killing him. I have no doubt that when the accusation became known, you made an effort to remember what I have just asked you, in order to disprove that ridiculous accusation."

Hammond's face brightened. "That's right, I did! Not that Mr. Wendell needed an alibi, you understand. It would have been beneath him even to offer an alibi."

"In other words," Clume said casually, "your memory of the facts made you realize that you couldn't have substantiated an alibi even if one had been needed."

"Well, I don't know about that. Mr. Wendell's movements that evening were the same as any other evening. His car was delivered at the curb at about five, and he left at the usual time. About a quarter past five."

"Ah! But how do you know that he didn't leave much later than that? Maybe he stayed in his office until as late as a quarter to six."

Hammond shook his head. "No, I remember when he left. It just happened that on that day I stayed in the office later than usual.

I didn't leave until half-past five."

"And when you got down to Broadway you say that Mr. Wendell's car was gone?"

"Yes, it was gone. But I didn't need that to know he had left. Just before he left, he came into the outer office where I was working and asked me to open the safe and let him have a hundred dollars. I gave him the bills, and he put them in his wallet and left through that door. Before I went out I went into his office and made sure his door was locked."

"Just one more mental test," Clume smiled. "When Mr. Wendell took the money from you, was he wearing his hat and overcoat?"

"Yes, he was."

"Now here's the last question and the hardest one. In what pocket did he carry his wallet?"

"Why, in his hip pocket, of course."

"And when he put away the bills you gave him, did he return the wallet to his hip pocket? There's one for you, Mr. Hammond!"

"And it's easy!" Hammond said triumphantly. "I'm very positive that he did *not* return it to his hip pocket. He put it in the side pocket of his overcoat. How do I remember that? Well, I remember thinking to myself that if I had a hundred dollars to carry around for pocket money, I wouldn't be so nonchalant about it."

The telephone rang.

"All right, Jordan," Bruce said into the mouthpiece. "I'll be ready for you by the time you get here. O.K."

He turned to Clume and asked if there were further questions Clume shook his head.

"That will be all then, Mr. Hammond. Many thanks to you for your cooperation. You can tell the young ladies from your office that I won't have to see them. I don't believe they'd be able to add anything to what you've told us."

"I'm sure they wouldn't. They left the office when I did."

He went out, followed by Jackson. Before the door closed again Lieutenant Jordan came in.

"I got the report from Dr. Dale," he said. "The bullet, entering the throat at a point just below the chin, ranged upward and lodged in the brain at the back of the head."

"Just as we thought," said Bruce. "That means that the murderer was holding the gun pointing upward."

To Clume he added, "That doesn't look good for the girl. She's not much over five feet two."

"There are other ways to explain the upward course of the bullet,"

Clume returned. "Was the gun fired at close range, Lieutenant?"

"There weren't any powder marks on the skin."

"Which only means that the gun was fired from a distance of more than several inches."

"That's right. Now let me tell you something interesting, Captain. I compared the bullet from Wendell's body with the two that killed Vincent Creel. All of them were fired from the same gun!"

"The same gun!" cried Bruce.

"Without question," said Jordan. "The bullets are identically marked, and they match the gun barrel."

Clume said cheerfully, "There goes the case against Margaret Embry, Captain."

"We'll know more about that when we trace the gun. It's a Wendell automatic, and Peterkin went out to the plant to check the number. Got anything about those fingerprints, Jordan?"

"Not yet. I'm going back now and work on them. Just to make a guess, I'd say that they aren't the girl's."

Bruce sighed. "So much the better. She's told a good story about how blood got on her fingers."

As Jordan left the office, the telephone rang. Bruce listened, saying "yeah" at intervals.

When he hung up the receiver, he told us, "That was Peterkin, phoning from the powder plant. The gun was made in January, '32. There's no record of its sale to any jobber or dealer. If you'd believe the records, it's still in stock out there." He ran his fingers through his sandy hair. "This is the damnedest case! I never saw the gun that couldn't be traced."

"You've traced this one," said Clume. "You just don't like the answer."

"I guess you're right," Bruce said wearily. "It must have been stolen from the factory. Frankly, I *don't* like the answer. If that was Wendell's gun, I'd have to believe that he shot Vincent Creel. I know that you have thought so all along, but I can't believe it. In the first place, we've very definitely established that there's no possible connection between Wendell and Creel. There's no possible motive, and there's no such thing as murder without motive."

Clume got the same feeling that came to me, that Bruce had had enough of us. Clume rose and put on his topcoat. He held out his hand to Bruce.

"Thank you, Captain. I appreciate your friendliness and I'm glad to have had this chance to know you better."

"I'm glad you were here," Bruce replied. "I know you're interested in the Embry family and I wanted you to see that I was giving the girl a square deal."

Clume said, "Let me make myself clear. I'm interested in them because I'm interested in solving this case and for no other reason. Will you keep me posted on any new developments? If it's something that's not for publication, just say so. I'll respect your wishes."

"You can count on me," promised the Captain, walking with us to the door.

Clume went out, and I stayed a moment to shakes Bruce's hand. "Thanks," I said. "It was like old times."

He looked down the hallway at Clume's retreating figure.

"You were right, Red," he told me. "That guy's a wonder!"

 **CHAPTER 13**

BOLEY HAD AN extra on the street by the time we left the police station. It was the late final with the front page made over, but it was being bought up as fast as the shouting newsies could hand it out. Their strident voices, calling "Extry! extry! Thomas Wendell murdered!" rang through the streets; the air was electric with excitement.

"We'll call on the Embrys this evening," Clume said. "Let's have our dinner first."

We went to Jobelman's where the headwaiter, who was also the proprietor, seated us in a booth that afforded a measure of privacy.

When we had finished our meal and lighted our cigarettes, Clume looked at his watch and asked, "Will you call the Embrys and tell them we'd like to come out for a little while? Tell them we'll be there at eight-thirty?"

When I got back to the table, Clume said, "I want to talk to them about that gun, Rufus. The district attorney isn't going to overlook the fact that the gun was taken from the factory at a time when Margaret and her father were employed there. He'll find it difficult, if not impossible, to prove that either of them took it; but that won't stop him when the public begins to clamor for action. The public wasn't especially interested in the murder of a tramp and cared very little whether or not the case was ever solved. But the murder of Thomas Wendell is another matter. The public will demand an arrest; and when the time comes, if no other suspect is available, Margaret Embry will be the victim."

The shadow that hung over the Embry home had deepened. The last time Clume and I had sat in the living room, the atmosphere was that of a home in which some member of the family was gravely ill. Tonight it was like returning after the patient had died.

Peggy was in bed, and Clume said she needn't be disturbed.

"I'm glad of that," Mrs. Embry said. "The poor child is exhausted — Mr. Clume, what is going to happen to us? It looks as if God is punishing us. And I don't know why we should be punished."

"That's the thought that always accompanies adversity," Clume answered. "When misfortune strikes, we cry, 'Why has this happened to me?' That thought is more crushing than the blow that inspires it."

Mrs. Embry, seated on the divan beside her husband, twisted her handkerchief into a linen rope.

"But what are we to think? Our lives were so peaceful until that evening when I saw — when I thought I saw — "

"You *thought* you saw?"

She shuddered. "I don't know what to say now. And it doesn't matter any more. If only I hadn't been looking out of the window, then none of this would have happened."

Clume shook his head. "You're mistaken, Mrs. Embry. It would have happened anyway. The tramp would have been shot; Wendell would have been killed."

She started to speak, but Clume stopped her with a wave of his hand. He was plainly impatient with her.

"Listen to me carefully. The district attorney may find it expedient to build up a case against your daughter directly, and against you and Mr. Embry indirectly. He will have to connect the murder of the tramp with the murder of Wendell, for they are unmistakably related. The same gun that was used to kill the tramp was used to kill Wendell."

Oliver Embry, who had been sitting back in apathetic silence, was roused to sudden interest.

"The same gun, Mr. Clume?" he exclaimed. "That makes my wife's story even more incredible."

"That's what I was about to say," said Clume. "The police have never believed Mrs. Embry's story. After finding the gun that killed both victims, they are less likely than ever to believe it." He looked at Mrs. Embry. "And if you retract your story at this late date, they are going to wonder whether the discovery of the gun has anything to do with your change of mind — or change of heart."

She was disconcerted by his annoyance.

"I — I didn't say I was going to retract my story, Mr. Clume. I only said —"

"You are unshaken in your belief that it was Wendell?"

"Yes, I am!"

"I don't approve of that," Oliver Embry said with surprising force. "I don't approve of it at all, Mr. Clume. From the very beginning I've thought that my wife was mistaken. You know that. And I think that this second murder proves it. Just before you came this evening, I was trying to persuade her —"

"So that's it!" said Clume.

"Yes. I'm responsible for her change of heart. And I don't like Peggy's story about seeing a man leave Mr. Wendell's office. I don't like it at all. I don't see why women have to talk so much! It only gets all of us deeper and deeper into trouble. Can't they learn that the less they say, the better off they are?"

Clume listened quietly, and though he didn't manifest surprise at Embry's show of spirit, I knew that he must have felt it.

"But what if your wife and daughter told the truth?"

"Even so," Oliver Embry returned warmly. "We'd avoid all this torture if they didn't talk so much!"

Clume shook his head sadly. "What fools ye mortals be! I suppose you don't consider it talking too much when you make these statements? But if the district attorney were sitting here now, he would begin to get notions — false notions, no doubt, but certain ideas, nevertheless. He would wonder, perhaps, whether your daughter wasn't lying in order to protect someone. Criminologists know that women will resort to falsehood more readily in defense of someone else than in defense of themselves. From there, he may be led to wonder just where you were when the tramp was shot to death."

Embry's sallow face grew waxen. He lifted both hands as if to ward off a blow.

"He knows where I was! I was on the bus on my way home. I was with Peggy."

"But your daughter is the only one who can substantiate your alibi. And if she is not to be believed in one matter, who shall take her word in another?"

"Mr. Clume!" He fairly moaned the name. "You don't think —"

"I'm not saying what *I* think," Clume said mercilessly, "but what the district attorney might think. He might also wonder where you were when Wendell was killed this afternoon. I suppose you were here between five-thirty and six-thirty. In that event, you have only your wife to substantiate your alibi. And if her testimony is not to be trusted — Well, you see how it goes, Mr. Embry. The criminal investigator has a cold, calculating, impersonal mind. It's quite necessary."

For a moment Oliver Embry sat with his hands covering his face. Mrs. Embry laid her hand on his shoulder and looked pleadingly at Clume.

"The district attorney wouldn't think such things," she said. "Not for a minute could he suspect that Oliver had anything to do with these terrible crimes."

Embry removed his hands from his face and clasped them convulsively between his knees.

"You're wrong about that, Jane," he declared somewhat wildly. "The police have a way of suspecting everybody. No one escapes them, once they get started. Everybody is guilty until he can prove his innocence." He turned to Clume. "Isn't that what you mean, Mr. Clume? Isn't that what you're warning me against?"

"I'm not warning you," said Clume; "I'm reproving you, as I had occasion to do once before and with respect to the same thing. I'm trying to show you that by influencing your wife you are inviting trouble. Both she and Peggy must tell the truth and stick to it through thick and thin. They must not change their stories because you happen not to approve of them. Would you want the police to doubt Peggy if she should be called on to testify that you were on the bus with her when the tramp was shot? Would you want them to doubt your wife if she should have to testify that you were in this house between four-thirty and five-thirty this afternoon?"

"That's just it," he said hollowly. "I wasn't. I wasn't at home then."

"You weren't?" Clume asked calmly. "Where were you?"

"I was downtown. I didn't get home until just before six."

Clume waved his hand, as if the matter were of no consequence.

"Don't let that worry you. It isn't likely that you'll be asked to account for your whereabouts. But if you were, there must be someone who can support your statements. Where were you at that time?"

Gone was the man's brief flash of spirit. His stark terror was more repulsive than his customary meek self-effacement.

"At a quarter past four I was at the Fairmont Trust Company."

"But the bank closed at three," Clume reminded gently.

"I had a special appointment down there with Mr. Watkins of the mortgage department. He asked me to call at that hour. I have the letter he wrote me."

"Well?"

"I was there transacting business until about half past four; maybe twenty to five. When I left there, I walked over to Broadway to get the bus. But when I got to Seventh and Broadway I decided to walk part of the way. I walked up Broadway to Eighteenth and then north on Eighteenth, following the bus route. I got on a bus at Eighteenth and Oak Hill."

"What time was that?"

"I don't know exactly. But since I got home at a quarter to six, I should say that it was around five-twenty-five or five-thirty."

"Did you meet anyone you know?"

"No."

Clume was silent a while, stroking his nose meditatively.

"I'm afraid we've side-tracked the conversation," he said at length, "and it's my fault. I came to talk about your daughter's predicament and, instead of adding to your distress, I wanted to put your minds at ease. Margaret is the suspect; not you, Mr. Embry. I don't believe that she's in any great peril; that is, she isn't going to be convicted of a crime she didn't commit. But she's in for all of the unpleasantness that Mrs. Embry has been experiencing — the repeated questioning, and so forth. And she may even be brought to trial."

Mr. Embry seemed not to be listening. He sat hunched forward with his hands dangling between his scrawny knees. Mrs. Embry unrolled her twisted handkerchief and wiped tears from her cheeks.

"Poor child!" she murmured. "Poor child!"

"Yes, it's a pity," said Clume, "but it's inevitable. However, it's the final outcome that matters, and you needn't worry about that. You see, the police have the gun, and through that they'll trace the murderer."

I knew why Clume made that doubtful assertion and I looked quickly at Mr. and Mrs. Embry. I caught no change in their expressions. Mrs. Embry, perhaps, brightened the least bit, and Mr. Embry's face remained a mask of abject despair.

Clume sat up, looked at his watch, and hitched back his chair a little. I knew that that was that. A moment later, he rose.

CHAPTER 14

ON FRIDAY MORNING I covered Wendell's funeral. I don't like being flippant about death, but those grand-scale funerals always make me sardonic. And make no mistake: Wendell's funeral was on a grand scale. By proclamation of the mayor, all public offices, banks, and business firms suspended activity between ten and twelve. There wasn't much difference between that day and the Fourth of July or Armistice Day except for the merest implication of solemnity in the flags that hung at half mast.

At one-thirty I rushed back to the city room and dashed out a story that mentioned none of the things that were uppermost in my mind. I'm telling them now.

When I finished my story, I gave it to Boley.

"Thank God," I said, "that Wendell had only one life to lay down for his country. Is Clume in his office?"

"He's at the d. a.'s office," Boley told me. "He said you should join him there when you finished the story." He picked up my manuscript and a blue pencil, ready to get to work on it. "We ought to be ashamed of ourselves, giving so much space to this hokus-pokus. You know what all the shooting's for, don't you? It's the old city hall gang trying to repair the damage done by Wendell's death. The king is dead — but may his policies, and politics, rule forever!"

I hurried over to the Criminal Courts Building.

Miss Fleming said, "Go right in; you're expected," and I walked into the rear office.

Clume, Bruce, and Cook were sitting in there in an atmosphere of sympathetic friendliness. They wore serious expressions, but the erstwhile coldness and hostility were noticeably absent. Bruce and the d. a. nodded to me as I entered.

When I had taken a chair, Clume turned to me and said, "We've been discussing the murder, especially the implication of Margaret Embry. Mr. Cook is of the opinion that the evidence against the girl justifies some immediate action; and though I can appreciate his point of view, I can't entirely agree with it. I was about to explain to these gentlemen the theory you advanced to me last night. As I told you then, I believe that Mr. Cook and Captain Bruce should be given the opportunity to consider it."

I'll give myself credit; I didn't bat an eye. I said:

"You know how I feel about it, Mr. Clume."

He nodded. "Do you want to tell them — or shall I?"

"Go ahead," I said largely, "if you don't mind."

He turned to them, settling himself in his chair. No matter with what interest they awaited his words, they were positively bored compared with me. What in the world was he up to? What was this important theory of mine which I was about to hear for the first time? I tried not to look too interested, but I believe it was lucky that their eyes were on Clume when he began to speak; for my surprise and consternation were so great that they must have shown on my face. Clume was telling them about Oliver Embry!

He built up a case against the man that was cold-bloodedly damning. He began with the suggestion that Embry might have stolen the revolver a year ago when the family moved to Walker Street. No one knew, he pointed out, at what time Embry arrived at home on the evening of Creel's murder, nor that he and Peggy had come home together. All we knew was that they had appeared at the front door together while the police were questioning Mrs. Embry.

He mentioned the gun again, pointing out that the murderer of Creel probably had retained it until he had used it on Wendell — the gun that had been stolen from the factory. Then he spoke of Embry's lack of an alibi for Wednesday afternoon between four-thirty and five-thirty.

And in conclusion, "Mr. Reed told me this ponderable theory last night," he said, "and I'm passing it on to you, for whatever it may be worth. I forgot to mention one more point that Mr. Reed included. I'll put it in the form of a question. If Margaret Embry had seen her father leave Wendell's office, or, having walked in, had suspected that her father had been there ahead of her, wouldn't she be likely to make up her story about the tramp who walked with a limp?"

He stopped, and I gripped the arms of my chair with all my strength in an effort to maintain a placid face. I was furiously indignant, not only because he had passed the buck to me, but because of his perfidy to the Embrys who trusted him so completely.

Both Bruce and the d. a. accepted the theory in a big way. The longer they discussed it, the more tenable it seemed to them. Captain Bruce, noticing the fiery color of my face, grinned at me across the room and said:

"You needn't sit there blushing like a schoolgirl, Red. You've done a first-rate piece of deduction. We never gave a thought to the old man. I guess tagging around after me gave you good training. We'll give you credit."

"Keep it," I returned with an ill-humor that must have surprised him. "I don't want my named mixed up in it."

"We'll consider this strictly confidential, Reed," Cook hastened to assure me. "We just want you to know that we appreciate your cooperation. I suppose there will be many opportunities for us to return the favor."

This outpouring of the milk of human kindness and the hearty handclasps that went around as we took our leave gave me insight into the reason for Clume's outrageous action. I felt that it was goodwill purchased at too high a price.

I couldn't speak my mind until Clume and I went into his office and closed the door. Then I exploded. He sat in his chair, and I stood looking down at him furiously.

"I'm quitting! I'm through!"

"Quitting?" he returned mildly. "I thought you appeared a bit annoyed about something, but I didn't think it was that serious."

"Of all the rotten tricks I ever saw, yours was the worst. To pull a stunt like that on people who trust in you as the best friend — the only friend — they have in the world. I can't understand it."

"That's the trouble, Rufus; you can't understand it. Suppose you sit down, and we'll take the back cover off the watch and let you see how it works. So far, you've only heard it ticking."

I flung myself into a chair.

"That's better," he said, fixing himself more comfortably. "It distresses the back of my neck to look up as I talk. Now let me explain, and then you may not want to walk out on the first act of what promises to be an interesting show. By the way; why do you think I pulled this stunt, as you put it? Have you any idea?"

"Of course I have. You want to warm up to the d. a."

He smiled faintly. "I was thinking how helpful it would be if Bruce and the district attorney were to evolve the theory that Mr. Embry might be the guilty one. From there it was but a step to the decision to give them the theory myself."

"But how is it helpful to get Mr. Embry in trouble? Aren't they in deep enough without that?"

"They were in too deeply without that," he replied. "Our discussion the other night made me realize that Margaret Embry was the anointed lamb for the sacrificial altar. She was a suspect; and that is serious. She was the *only* suspect; and that is fatal. Consider, Rufus: In the bag of tricks of the criminal lawyer, none is so valuable as the juggling act known as injecting into the case the element of reasonable doubt. When the evidence is strong against the defendant, and the rebuttal is weak, the shrewd defense lawyer reaches into his bag and brings forth as many bewildering balls of doubt as possible. Since he can't prove that the defendant did not commit the crime, he tries to show that someone else might have committed it. While the prosecution is presenting its case, the jury watches only one ball that is tossed into the air. There is nothing confusing about that. But when the defense adds one ball after another, keeping most of them in the air at the same time, the minds of the jury become more and more confused until they can't distinguish one ball from another. If the evidence shows that only one person committed the crime, it is logical to believe that person guilty. But if two or more persons may have committed the crime, each one independent of the other, it is difficult to decide which one is guilty."

He paused; and by this time my wrath had melted away, and I felt more than a little ashamed of myself.

I said contritely, "I get you now, Mr. Clume. You were giving them something to think about besides Peggy."

"Exactly. They think that you and I have helped them. Actually, we've tied their hands for a while. We've given them the dilemma of the lover in the presence of both of the objects of his affection. Before very long they will be sadly reflecting how very pleasant life would be with either, if one of the fair charmers were away. They can't have both of them. They must accuse either one or the other. How can they work up a strong case against Peggy when her father might be guilty? And vice versa." He paused to chuckle quietly.

CHAPTER 15

THE BIG BREAK came on Monday morning. I was in Bruce's office at eight-thirty, having dropped in on my way to the city room to see whether the captain's gratitude was getting frayed at the ends. I knew that he and Cook had been working on both Peggy and her father over the week-end; but the Embrys were now veterans who knew how to take care of themselves in a battle, and Bruce and the d. a. found themselves just where they started.

"The only thing against the old man is his lack of an alibi," said

Bruce. "And, of course, the same motive that could be applied to the girl could also be applied to her father. But you have to prove more than opportunity and motive to convict a person of murder."

"I guess my theory wasn't so hot," I said apologetically. "But it looked queer to me that he didn't have an alibi and was so near the Wendell Building at the time of the murder."

"It was worth looking into," he told me. "We soon saw that it was full of holes, but in police work you've got to investigate every possible lead. The biggest flaw in the case against the old man is that his wife went to the d. a. with her story. If she knew or suspected that he killed Creel, she would have kept her mouth shut. Well, it's all in a day's work."

The door opened, and Jordan came in. He gave me a nod and spoke to Bruce.

"We got something on those fingerprints we found in Wendell's office, Captain. Just heard from the FBI. I wasn't hoping for results, but I sent them to Washington, anyway. And damned if they didn't have them on file." He read from the report in his hand. 'Name, Giles Jetty. Prints taken June 12th, 1917, at Chicago. Age, 28. Height, five-nine; hair, brown; eyes, brown. Charged with passing the queer — two fivers and a ten — on Chicago merchants. No previous record. Paroled to join the army.' " He looked up. "I've already wired to Chicago for information and to the War Department at Washington. We'll soon have more dope on this man."

Bruce reached for the telephone and scooped up the receiver. A moment later he was telling the d. a. all about it.

When he was through, Jordan went out; and Bruce said to me, "I'm asking you not to print any of this, Red. I can't let you use it until I give it to the other papers. That's the bargain I made with Asaph Clume. You two can be in on the ground floor, but not as newspapermen."

"I understand that," I said. "So the Embry girl was telling the truth after all! And Clume was the only one who believed it."

He shrugged. "Anyone has a fifty-fifty chance of being right on a guess like that. You either believe it or you don't. He believed Mrs. Embry's story, too, and you'll see that he's wrong on that one. Wait until we pick up this Giles Jetty. We *know* he killed Wendell, and I believe he killed Creel, too. Look here. The Embry girl didn't get a good look at him, but she said he was medium height, kind of stout, had broad shoulders, and walked with a limp. Add to that the FBI description that he has brown hair and brown eyes and you've got a rough description of Thomas Wendell. If Mrs. Embry saw Giles Jetty that evening, she could easily have mistaken him for Wendell, even if the two men don't actually look alike. Only a general physical resemblance would be necessary."

I hurried to the city room to tell Clume the news, and then remembered that he was attending a party powwow and probably wouldn't show up until noon. I went to work on my column. Heading it "Patience, please!" I dealt with the topic of the day, the investigation of Wendell's murder. I praised the efficiency of the district attorney and Captain Bruce, chief of the homicide bureau, and reminded the public that there was more to criminal investigation than just going out and nabbing the guilty man. I urged my readers to be patient until there came a break in the case and I sagely predicted that there would soon be a break.

The column finished, I put the copy on Clume's desk and returned to my own, picking up a copy of the *Times* on the way. Oliver Embry had followed his wife and daughter to the front page. Over his picture was the caption "Quizzed By Police." I thought, poor old Milquetoast! How he must yearn for mediocrity!

I yawned and glanced at the clock. It was ten-forty. I returned to the paper, and my eye lighted on a small head over a twenty line UP dispatch that had been used as a filler: RIVER VICTIM MAY BE MISSING TENNESSEAN. I began to read it idly when the sight of a name shocked me to attention. This is what I read:

FRANKLIN, Tenn., Oct. 29 (UP).—Believing that the body found this morning in Little Harpeth River by several negro children may be that of Giles Jetty, police summoned Mrs. Jetty to attempt identification. The body had been in the water for several weeks, and it is believed that identification will prove difficult.

Giles Jetty, forty-four-year-old Williamson County farmer, disappeared mysteriously September 25 when he drove a truckload of sheep to Franklin. When he failed to return to his farm, a search was instituted, the truck later being found on a road five miles east of Franklin. No trace of Jetty has been found.

That night I left Fairmont on the L. & N., southbound for Nashville. There was the possibility that I was off on a wild goose chase, but Clume and I agreed that the factors justified our conclusion that the Tennessee farmer was the man who left his fingerprints in Wendell's office. Giles Jetty was an uncommon name. His age, according to the UP dispatch, was forty-four, so that he was twenty-eight in 1917. He had disappeared from his community on September twenty-fifth, just two weeks before the murder of Vincent Creel.

I got to Franklin via Nashville where I hired a car and driver for the day. Franklin lay twenty miles to the south, and we sped over a wide paved highway through low wooded hills.

We stopped at Franklin to inquire the way to Giles Jetty's farm; then drove several miles east on a winding dirt road. The Jetty home stood far back from the road, a tall, square house of red brick, surrounded by giant oaks and maples. Around the house, chickens walked in the high fading grass, and several large lean dogs dozed in the sun on the uncovered stoop at the front door.

A negro came into view from around the side of the house. My driver hailed him.

"Hey, Sam! Is this here the Jetty place?"

The colored man shuffled toward us, pausing to pick up a clod of earth and throw it at the dogs, rooting them from the stoop.

"This is Jetty's," he said; "but Mist' Giles ain't hum. Been gone five weeks terday, and nobody don't know whar he's at. Jes' lak de arth swaller him up."

"Is Mrs. Jetty at home?" I asked.

"Yassuh, Mis' Sarah's hum. You wants to see Mis' Sarah, jes' knock on de do' yondah."

I got out of the car and rapped on the heavy weather-stained door. It was opened by a woman of about forty, tall and slender, with dark eyes and long dark hair that she wore piled up on top of her head. When I told her I was a reporter and wanted to talk with her about the disappearance of her husband, she asked me to come in. I followed her through a long narrow hall into a high-ceilinged living room where a log fire burned in the open fireplace, and the sun streamed in through tall windows.

"I'm not keen about the publicity," she said, after we were seated on the divan facing the fireplace. "Will you have to write this up and attract a lot of attention?"

When I hesitated to reply, she added, a pleading note in her voice, "You see, it's not as if I thought Mr. Jetty had met with foul play. I don't think he did, and the police agree with me. The fact is, I think he — he just deserted us. Now you know how I feel about publicity. I'm thinking of the children as well as myself."

"I understand that, Mrs. Jetty," I said sympathetically. "And let me make my position clear. I'm more interested in helping to find your husband than in getting a story for my paper. I want you to know that, so you won't be afraid to talk to me. I won't publish a word of it, if you don't want me to — at least not until some future development makes it necessary to publish it. In agreeing to that, I can speak for my editor as well as for myself."

"That's mighty kind of you," she said gratefully. "Are you on the *Banner* or the *Tennessean?*"

"I'm not from Nashville. I'm with a Fairmont paper."

As I spoke the name of my city, I watched her face carefully; but beyond a mild surprise that I had come so great a distance, her expression did not change. I showed her the item I had clipped from the *Times*.

"And you came all that distance!" she said as if the ways of newspapermen were past her understanding. "Whoever wrote this didn't get the facts straight. I wasn't asked to identify the body they found in the river. If it had been Mr. Jetty, the police would know it, no matter what condition the body was in. My husband was badly wounded in the war and has a number of scars on his body. They wouldn't need me to identify him."

She was silent a moment, looking past me out of the window. At length she returned her gaze to me.

"I told you that my husband deserted me. I'm afraid it wasn't fair to use that word. It must have given you the wrong impression. I don't want you to think that Mr. Jetty was the sort to leave his wife and children if he could help it."

"If he could help it?" I repeated.

"I mean, if he was — in his right mind." She sighed. "You can't very well understand without knowing all the circumstances. I told you that my husband was badly wounded in the war. For a while after he was brought into the field hospital near Chateau-Thierry the doctors didn't expect him to live. But he managed to hang on. Then they thought his mind was gone completely from shell-shock, but he fooled them again. He got all right — well — practically all right. We had a long fight, though, before he came through. He was in hospitals in France from March 1918 until April 1920. Then there was another year of hospitalization after we came back to this country."

"You were married before the war?"

"No, I first met my husband in the field hospital in France. I was a Red Cross nurse. We were married about six months before we returned to America. The twelfth of next month will be our fourteenth anniversary." She smiled sadly. "That was a real war romance, wasn't it? And we've been wonderfully happy. We have two children, a boy of ten and a girl of eight."

"Did your husband live here before the war?"

She shook her head. "He lived in Indiana. This was my father's place. My grandfather built the house eighty-five years ago with slave labor. I was born here and lived here all my life until I went into training. I was in a Nashville hospital when we entered the war and I volunteered for service overseas." She paused and added apologetically: "I'm afraid I'm talking in circles. Living out here, I don't often get a chance to talk to anyone."

I assured her of my interest.

"I inherited the place when my father died. That was shortly after my husband and I came back from France. Some tenants worked it until Mr. Jetty was well enough to leave the hospital, and then we moved here. It was a Godsend to have a place to come to and work for my husband to do."

"What did he do before the war?"

After a moment of troubled hesitation, Mrs. Jetty said, "'I don't know very much about Mr. Jetty's life before I met him. That isn't as strange as it sounds. My husband recovered his mind — that is, he was perfectly sane — but his memory was affected. Amnesia, you know. He couldn't remember anything of his past life. His memory began with his recovery of consciousness in the hospital."

"And all these years —"

"He never remembered. At first it bothered him terribly, and he would talk about trying to trace his past. But I always discouraged that."

"Why?"

"Well, I had already traced it. We had his home address; and when he was brought into the hospital, the war department notified his family. They never communicated with him as long as he was in France. Naturally, before I married him, I wanted to know something about him; but the only thing I really wanted to know was that he didn't already have a wife. Of course, he couldn't remember. But his enlistment papers had him down as unmarried and that was all that was necessary.

"'When we got back to America, I wrote a letter to his father, whose name was on the enlistment papers as closest relative. I wrote him a long letter, telling him about our marriage and explaining his son's condition and so forth. I told him that I wanted to know everything about my husband's past life so that I could try to waken his memory bit by bit. We were at a hospital in New Jersey at that time, and I suggested that the father come there to see his son, hoping that would help effect a cure."

"Did he come?"

"No. I received a letter from him telling me that I had made a terrible mistake in marrrying his son and that I'd live to regret it. He said that his son was a criminal and a disgrace to his family; that he had erased his name from the family Bible, and never wanted to see or hear of him again. You can imagine the shock that horrible letter gave me. I wasn't sorry that I'd married Mr. Jetty. I didn't care what he had been; his war record spoke for itself, and I'd lived with him long enough to know his fine qualities."

"So you never looked further into his past," I said.

"Yes, I did. About that time my father had a stroke and was about to die, and I came down here. On my way back, I stopped off in Fort Wayne and looked up my husband's people. I met his father and an older brother. His mother was dead, and there was a married sister living somewhere else. I didn't hear much about her, except that she shared the family's feelings toward my husband."

"Did you find out more about your husband?"

"A little. I found out enough to know that it wasn't as terrible as they made out. I think the older brother had a lot to do with keeping the hatred stirred up. They had a grain and feed business, and I think he wanted to inherit it. That was the impression I got. I'll always believe that Roger Jetty made things so unpleasant for my husband that he caused him to leave home in the first place. He went to Chicago in 1915, and it was there that he got into trouble."

She hesitated, then added, "I don't mind telling you what it was. He was arrested for passing counterfeit bills. I heard about it first from the father and later I looked up the records on it. They lead me to believe that the affair wasn't nearly as black as the father painted it. The records show that it was my husband's first offense, and there must have been other things in his favor because, although he was convicted, he was paroled to join the army."

She stopped, and for a while we were silent.

Then I said, "Mrs. Jetty, as a trained nurse you probably know pretty much about amnesia. In some cases, doesn't memory return?"

She nodded. "It usually does. Many people have a temporary forgetfulness that lasts only a few days. Sometimes the loss is permanent. It depends on what causes it."

"But in your husband's case it was permanent?"

"It looked that way after all these years. But you can never tell. I read of cases where memory returned after twenty years or more. I know what you're thinking and I thought of the same thing when my husband disappeared last month. I wondered whether he suddenly remembered and had gone back to Fort Wayne to look up his family. I telephoned and spoke to his brother. His father is dead. Roger Jetty told me that he hadn't seen or heard from my husband."

"What do you think now about the possibility of his having regained his memory?"

"I think it's the most likely explanation of his disappearance," she said. "Everything points to that. In the first place, he wasn't so well for several days before he disappeared. I mean, he had one of those spells that he had from time to time when he would get sort of moody and silent, just as if he were trying hard to remember something.

"On the day he disappeared, he seemed to be at the worst point of one of those spells. He had scarcely spoken to me or the children for at least twenty-four hours, and I didn't like the idea of his driving to Franklin with the truck. But when he's like that, the best thing to do is to let him alone.

"He took twelve head of sheep to market and sold them. Then he went to the bank and drew three hundred dollars. He must have already planned to leave because he drew that sum in addition to the money he had received for the sheep. Mr. Yost, who bought the sheep, and Mr. Pritchet at the bank, said that he acted very peculiar. Well, you know the rest. When he left the bank, he drove away and he hasn't been seen since."

"What puzzles me," I said, "is why he hasn't let you hear from him."

"Maybe he doesn't remember me," she replied. "Sometimes, when a victim of amnesia recovers his memory, it is just as if he woke up at the time of his accident. He remembers everything that happened before the injury, but nothing of what happened afterwards. He picks up life just where he left off, and everything else is like a forgotten dream."

"Is that always the case?"

"Not always. But it's possible."

"Then it doesn't look as if that happened to Mr. Jetty. If his memory suddenly returned after he left Franklin, he wouldn't have drawn that money from the bank. If it returned earlier and blotted out the past fifteen years, he wouldn't have remembered that he had money in the bank."

She listened with her head bowed, looking at her hands on her lap. For the first time she let her emotions escape her control and rise to the surface. I saw her blinking at the tears that welled into her eyes. I liked her and I felt sorry for her. Her present suffering was as nothing compared with what was in store for her. I thought, her father-in-law's prophecy will at last come to pass; she will regret her marriage when she learns that her husband is a murderer.

Before I took leave of her, she gave me a snapshot of her husband. She went outside with me to the stoop to bid me goodbye.

"Thank you for your interest, Mr. Reed. Somehow I have a feeling that you're going to help me."

"I'll do what I can," I said. I felt as I suppose a doctor must feel when he knows that his patient is doomed and tells the patient's wife that he'll "do everything possible."

"If I hear anything, I'll let you know," she said. "Maybe he'll write to me. Goodbye and — and good luck!"

Before returning to Fairmont, I followed my last remaining clue. I wired ahead to Henry Creel in Toledo, asking him to meet me at his hotel at six o'clock the next day, and he was waiting for me in his room when I got there. I showed him the snapshot of Giles Jetty.

"This man," I said, "was on the road between September 25th and October 9th. Do you recognize him?"

He shook his head, studying the picture. "Never saw him in my life."

"Couldn't your brother have met him? You and Vincent weren't together all the time, were you?"

"We were, during the two weeks before we hit Fairmont. I never met this guy and I'm sure that Vin didn't, either. Who is he?"

"He's one of the two men who might have killed your brother," I said, returning the picture to my wallet. "Thomas Wendell is the other. And you are positive that he didn't know either of them."

He frowned and scratched the back of his head. "It don't make sense."

I said, "Are you telling me?"

CHAPTER 16

I REPORTED TO Clume next morning and let him worry about it. Then I went to see Captain Bruce with the intention of letting him have the snapshot of Giles Jetty. It was Clume's idea, not mine. Perhaps his attitude toward scoops was very intelligent and mature, but it seemed to me that as long as we had spent time, money, and effort in order to get the dope on Jetty, we might as well get an exclusive story out of it. That morning the district attorney had called in reporters from the three papers and had released the story about the identification of the fingerprints. Larry Critchfield brought it in just as I left Clume's office. Either the police had learned practically nothing since Monday morning, or Cook was holding out on the press. In the typewritten statement he had handed out there was nothing new to show that Jetty had been traced to Tennessee; nothing, in fact, that I hadn't heard from Jordan Monday morning in Bruce's office.

Here was an opportunity to run a story that would make the other papers look silly. But Clume was overflowing with the milk of human kindness. He pointed out that it would make the police look even sillier.

"It wouldn't be fair play, Rufus. If Bruce hadn't let you be present when Jordan reported, that filler about Jetty wouldn't have given you a short cut."

"But, my God!" I cried. "If we don't take advantage of the breaks —"

"Not in this case at this time," he cut in with finality. "Anyway, we have already taken advantage of the break. We aren't dependent on the good-will of the district attorney; we have the facts. We can afford to be magnanimous."

So I went to see Bruce with the intention of giving him Jetty's picture, though I felt as magnanimous about it as the kid whose mother makes him share his ice cream with the little boy next door.

As soon as I entered his office, I noticed the change that had come over him. His greeting wasn't exactly unfriendly, but it decidedly lacked the warmth I expected. He gave me one of those cold-fish handshakes that make you sorry you didn't keep your hand in your pocket.

"I've been out of town since Monday night," I said. "Just got back this morning."

He fiddled with some papers on his desk.

"Critchfield said you were away. Have a nice trip?"

"Swell. What's been happening around here?"

He picked up a sheet of paper and began to read it. He was giving a perfect imitation of a busy executive trying to get rid of an insurance salesman.

"Nothing new. Not a thing," he replied, without looking at me.

I felt a warm wave of anger breaking over me.

"Does that mean you don't want to talk to me? If you're sore about something, say so."

He put aside the paper and looked up.

"Keep your shirt on, Red. I'm not sore about anything. I've got a lot of work to do and I'm trying to get to the point. The Wendell case is just where it was. We're looking for Jetty and hoping to pick him up soon. That's all I can tell you."

He glanced uneasily at the door. I saw the uneasiness in his eyes when he looked at me again.

"Be reasonable, Red." He was careful that his voice did not carry beyond the door. "You know where I stand. I like my job and I want to keep it. Mayor Scruggs gave it to me, and he can take it away any time he wants. I got hell yesterday for being too chummy with you and Clume. I think that someone on the *Times* or *Star-Herald* complained about it; said that I was playing favorites with Clume's paper. Anyway, I've got to be careful."

His explanation cooled me off a little.

"That suits me," I said. "I didn't come here to get information, but to give you some."

"What do you mean?"

"You can read about it in the *Express*," I said, walking out of the office.

Larry Critchfield was standing in the hall near the press room, and he gave me a sign. We went into the deserted press room and closed the door.

"I think something's up," he told me. "Lieutenant Jordan and Kelly left town early this morning. I don't know where they went, but I have a hunch it has something to do with the Wendell case."

"Did they go by train or automobile?"

"Train. I don't know much about it. I happened to overhear a remark that Peterkin made to the desk sergeant. He was peeved because he didn't get to go with Jordan instead of Kelly. They left at 6:45 this morning."

"That's the southbound L. & N.," I said. "They're going where I came from."

"That isn't all," he added. "I haven't seen Jimmy Nelson around this morning. I just called the *Star-Herald* and asked for him and their operator told me he was out of town. Do you know what I think? Bruce is trying to double-cross us."

"I wouldn't be surprised," I returned. "But he won't get away with it."

I was sure that Clume wouldn't feel so magnanimous when he

heard what they were trying to put over on us. For once, I thought I'd get my way. We had time to get the story into the city edition.

Our telephone switchboard was in the city room near the stairway

As I came up the steps, a few at a time, I heard the operator say "Here is Mr. Reed now! Hold the phone, please. I'll put him righ on." She called to me, "Mr. Reed, here's a long-distance call for you I'll put it on your telephone."

I went to my desk and grabbed the phone. After a moment th call came through, and I heard a woman's voice, vibrant with ex citement.

"I want Mr. Rufus Reed. Is that Mr. Reed?"

"This is Rufus Reed," I said. "Who's calling?"

"Oh, Mr. Reed! I've been trying to get you for an hour. This i Mrs. Jetty. Can you hear me?"

I told her I could hear perfectly.

"Mr. Reed, I want you to help me. Please listen carefully an decide what can be done. This morning I got a letter from a mai who used to live in Franklin. He said — but maybe it would b clearer if I read you the letter. I have it right here."

"Read it," I said.

"Dear Mrs. Jetty: I reckon you will be surprised to hear from m after all this time. As you know, we have settled in Kirkwood, Mis souri; and I am traveling for a St. Louis hardware concern. Mrs Olden misses you all and often talks about you. But here is what am writing you about. I arrived in Fairmont yesterday mornin, and registered at the Palace Hotel. Later on, I was in the downstair lobby when I seen a man sitting in a chair in the lobby. I could hav swore it was Mr. Jetty. I looked at him, and he looked at me but nc like he had ever seen me before. I went up to him and I said, 'Ain' you Giles Jetty?' but he just looked at me kind of funny like and sai nothing. So I said, 'I'm Sam Olden that used to live in Franklir Tennessee, don't you remember me?' He still didn't answer but jus got up and walked out of the hotel. I asked at the desk if Giles Jett was registered there and was told he was not. The clerk said the ma I spoke to was registered John Smith from Nashville. I did not se the man again before I left Fairmont last night and came here t Centerville; but the more I think about it, the more sure I am tha he was your husband. When you know a man for ten years like knew Giles Jetty, you ain't likely not to know him when you see hin Knowing about his old trouble, I am wondering if maybe somethin went wrong with him. If he is home with you, then I am wrong an no harm done. In which case he has a double that looks exactly lik him, even to the scar on his chin."

Mrs. Jetty stopped reading and said tensely, "Mr. Reed, that must have been my husband he saw. Sam Olden's letter was mailed yesterday morning from Centerville, so it was Tuesday morning when he saw Mr. Jetty. Maybe he's still at the Palace Hotel."

"I'll find out immediately," I said. "I'll phone you as soon as I know anything definite."

Without stopping to see Clume, I hurried away to the Palace Hotel. I was filled with excitement and a warm glow of triumph. If I worked fast and luck was with me, I would bag a story that any reporter would give his right arm for. My plan was to get hold of Jetty, keep him under cover until we brought out an extra, and then turn him over to Bruce. The *Star-Herald* was probably laughing at us now, but they wouldn't be laughing this evening. Their reporter, who had accompanied Jordan and Kelly to Tennessee, would telephone his intended scoop late tonight, and oh, how sick those boys in the city room would feel by that time! Bruce and Cook would be feeling pretty sick themselves, which made it all the merrier. They certainly had it coming to them.

The Palace Hotel was on Front Street, about a mile from the office. It was a cheap hotel, occupying an old building of red brick. In its small, tile-floored lobby were battered black leather chairs and brass cuspidors on rubber mats.

I went to the desk and asked for John Smith of Nashville. The clerk looked in a pigeonhole. The key was there.

"He's not in," he told me.

It was half-past twelve; there was nothing unusual about his not being in his room at this hour. But I had a sudden premonition of disaster.

"He hasn't checked out, has he?"

"No."

"What time did he go out this morning?"

"I don't know. His key was in the box when I came on an hour ago."

The number under the box was 221.

There was a chance that he was in his room, and I took the stairs to the second floor. I was about to knock on the door of 221 when a chambermaid came out of the next room.

"Nobody's in there," she said to me. "He ain't showed up since day before yesterday."

"Are you sure of that?"

"His bed wasn't slept in night before last or last night. I was just goin' to tell the manager."

I went downstairs and out to the street. There was no use in wait
ing around there; it was plain that Jetty, recognized by Sam Olden
had pulled up stakes and moved on.

Sick with disappointment, I stood for an undecided moment in
front of the hotel. I was about to walk away when a colored bell hop
called to me from the door.

"Was you lookin' for the man in 221?"

"Yes," I said. "Do you know where he is?"

He grinned. "I reckon I do. He got pinched."

"Pinched!"

"Tha's what."

"How do you know?"

"I see him. It was long 'bout ten o'clock Tuesday mawnin'. I was
standin' right out there front o' the do', and out comes this here
Mr. 221 and walks off down the street. Ain't gone but a little ways
when two men they looked like dicks comes up to him and stahts
talkin'. Then off they goes with Mr. 221 between them and they gits
into a police cah and drives off."

"Didn't you tell the clerk about it?"

"I tol' the manager. It's all the same to him. Mr. 221 come in with
out no luggage so he paid every day in advance."

"Do you remember the dicks who pinched him?" I asked. "What
did they look like?"

"Well, one was a tall guy and the other was short and heavy."

I gave the boy half a dollar and made tracks for the office. I
burned up that mile in next to nothing, and it's a wonder I didn't
have a squad of cops at my heels. I was so winded when I burst into
Clume's office that I could hardly tell him the news. Finally I managed to get it out.

"They've captured Jetty!" I panted. "And we're the only paper in
town that knows it!"

 **CHAPTER 17**

I TOLD CLUME the whole story, and though he heard me with interest, he showed no particular enthusiasm.

"It's too bad I didn't get hold of Jetty before Peterkin and Kelly nabbed him," I concluded; "but we've got a hot story anyway. But we've got to work fast. I believe that the *Star-Herald* will wait until they hear from Jimmy Nelson about seven tonight; but they may decide to spring the story about Jetty's capture in an early extra, and then follow it up with the story that Nelson phones in from Franklin. If we don't scoop them on this, Mr. Clume, I'll never be able to hold my head up."

He sat slouched in his chair, stroking his nose.

After a while he looked at me and asked, "You're quite sure that the bell hop's story is true?"

"True!" I cried. "How could it be phony? Doesn't it stack up perfectly with what we know? That boy had no ax to grind by lying to me. He described the men who picked up Jetty as a tall man and a short heavy one. That's the team of Peterkin and Kelly. I'm so positive of that, I'm going to credit them with the arrest in my story."

"That was day before yesterday. I'm trying to figure out why the capture wasn't made public. Why are they keeping him under cover? You say that Jordan and Kelly left only this morning, presumably bound for Jetty's home. If they have Jetty in jail, what is the reason for going down there?"

I answered quickly, "To check up. Jetty probably won't talk. From other sources they learn his background. So they —"

"That's reasonable," he cut in, nodding slowly. "But I don't understand why they haven't announced his capture. It's very odd. The usual procedure is to tell the public about every suspect they get their hands on."

In my desperation to win him over, I found an answer.

"Maybe I was wrong when I said he wouldn't talk. Maybe he *did* talk — and they didn't like what he said! Sooner or later they'd have to make it public; but they'd like to hold it until after Tuesday's election. This is our big chance to force their hand. No matter what it is, they'll have to come out with it. What do you say, Mr. Clume? Do we get out that extra?"

For a moment he looked at me, his lips pursed, his eyes clouded by indecision. Then he sat up and hit the arm of his chair with the flat of his hand.

"Send Boley in here!" he said. "And get to work on that story!"

I went to my desk and got to work. The story poured out as fast as my fingers could tap the keys. It was a natural. It had everything a big story should have, and every word of it was a beat. I made it plain that it was a beat; that the *Express* had uncovered the facts in spite of an official effort to keep the public in the dark. I pointed out that only a few hours earlier the district attorney's office had announced that the bloody fingerprints found on Wendell's desk belonged to an ex-convict named Giles Jetty, whom the police were seeking, but that actually the suspected murderer was in the county jail where he had been secretly held since his arrest Tuesday morning.

I realized that I could grow old in a city room without getting another opportunity like this and I made the most of it. I told everything there was to tell and I laid it on thick. When I finished and read through the copy, I was delightfully surprised to discover that I was a master of innuendo. Without coming right out and saying so, I made it appear that everyone in the other camp, from Mrs. Wendell down to Detectives Peterkin and Kelly, was in a vile conspiracy to keep the public uninformed or misinformed. As for the *Times* and the *Star-Herald*, they were either parties to the conspiracy or else incapable of supplying the news.

When I left my desk with a handful of copy, I was suddenly aware that the city room was in the state of turmoil that precedes rushing out an extra. I caught sight of Dan O'Malley of the composing room, standing at Boley's desk. Boley's green eyeshade was awry, and he looked as if he had come into the Promised Land.

I went into Clume's office and handed him my copy, sinking into a chair to await his reading. He read with amazing rapidity, seeming to take in an entire page with a single downward sweep of his eyes. When he had finished, he looked up and for a moment stared vacantly past me. There was a frown between his eyes.

I asked fearfully, "Don't you like it?"

He roused himself, wrote his O. K. on the first page, and handed the manuscript to me across the desk.

"It's very good," he said. "Take it to Boley."

It was twenty minutes to two, and my stomach was reminding me that I hadn't eaten since an early breakfast on the train. Ahead of me lay the unpleasant task of telephoning Mrs. Jetty, who was waiting for my call; but that must be postponed until our extra was on the street. If I spoke to her now, she might telephone or telegraph police headquarters and spill the beans.

I went around the corner to Bernie's. At a table near the door sat three *Star-Herald* men, Jack Brinley, who covered the State House and political news in general; Fred Davis, who wrote sports; and a cub whose name I couldn't remember. Brinley was about forty-five, and he liked to consider himself the dean of reporters in Fairmont.

When I was with the *Times* he had been friendly to me in his patron-
izing way. Since I worked for the *Express* and covered the same territory he covered, he had found delight in riding me, especially when
other reporters were around. He did it always with an eye out for
my heft and my red hair, never going far enough to justify my taking a swing at him.

The men greeted me when I came in, and Brinley asked me to sit
with them. I took the fourth chair and gave my order,

"My God!" said Davis who had a sandwich and a glass of beer in
front of him. "Do you put that much away every lunch?"

"I'm starved," I said. "I had breakfast before six o'clock on the
train."

"Where were you?" Davis asked.

"Off on a story."

Brinley grinned and gave them a wink.

"Red went to Washington to interview Roosevelt. He sent for
you, didn't he, Red?"

"Hell, no!" I said. "When I want to interview the President, I
send for him."

"You should have been in town to cover the rally at the Auditor-
ium last night," Brinley said. "I could have got you in, even if you
are on the *Express*. Your rag didn't even have a man there. Can you
imagine a paper getting scooped on a political rally?"

Davis said, "That's nothing. You can scoop the *Express* with the
final score of a football game."

The waiter brought my lunch, and I went to work on it. For once
I welcomed their bantering, for I knew that at that very moment our
presses were spitting out an edition that would make newspaper his-
tory. When they saw that they weren't getting a rise out of me, they
changed the subject. Davis began to talk about Fairmont University's prospects of winning the Conference football title. Then Brinley, as usual, switched the talk to politics. Next Tuesday's vote, he
predicted, would be the heaviest on record for an off-year election.
It would be a landslide for the machine. He turned to me.

"I guess your boss thought that when Wendell was bumped off,
the machine would fall to pieces. He'll feel pretty sick when the re-
turns are in Tuesday night."

"But Mr. Brinley," I said humbly, "we probably won't hear about
it until Wednesday noon."

Brinley had talked himself into a serious mood.

He said earnestly, "No fooling, Red. You're too good a man to
waste your time on the *Express*. Clume isn't a newspaper man; he's

a blue-nose reformer. He was all right in the old days. Then he stood in with Arnold Wendell, and whoever is on the side of the Wendell family can bask in the reflected glory. He made the mistake of his life when he broke with Thomas Wendell. He thought he could do it because he mistook reflected light for the spotlight. He moved away, but the spotlight stayed where it belonged — on the Wendells. For twelve years now he's been butting his head against a stone wall; and the only reason he doesn't knock his brains out is because he hasn't got any. His sheet is a joke, and everybody who works on it gets to be a joke, too."

"There's a laugh for every joke, isn't there?" I said.

"A laugh?"

"Sure. And did you ever hear what they say about the last laugh?"

"You'll never get it by working for the *Express*. Nobody can live that long."

Glancing out of the window, I saw three of our empty route trucks go past, in the direction of our building. A moment later a gang of boys went by on the run. My heart thumped. The extra must be about ready for the street.

"Listen, Brinley," I said. "I'll make a bet with you. I'll bet you fifty bucks, even money, that we score the next big beat made in this town."

The three men looked at me incredulously. Then they looked at each other, and I perceived their silent communication. I knew what it was. They were reminding each other that Jimmy Nelson was now on the train with Jordan and Kelly and at about seven-thirty tonight would phone in an exclusive story from Franklin, Tennessee.

Almost simultaneously, Davis and Brinley shouted, "I'll take that bet!"

And the cub said dolefully, "If only I had fifty smackers —"

Brinley said, "I saw this sucker first, Fred! It's my fifty!"

"Don't fight about it, fellows," I said. "I'll take you both on at fifty each."

The cub was whining, "If only I had fifty smackers."

"Don't cry, kid," I told him. "I'll take you on for five."

He brightened a little.

"Well, five is better than nothing."

We shook hands across the table. I called the waiter, paid my check, and got up.

Brinley said, "Count out your pennies, Red, and have the dough ready at noon tomorrow. We'll be waiting for you right here. The pay-off is coming sooner than you expect."

"Not sooner than *I* expect," I replied. "That's a date. Here at noon tomorrow."

Too late, Brinley got a hunch. He narrowed his eyes.

He said portentously, "I wonder if this guy has put something over on us."

I grinned down at them. From a distance came the shrill sing-song call of a boy. I listened; and when it came again, it was a little nearer. It was still a song without words but it was the sweetest music I ever heard. The extra was on the street!

I said, "Don't forget, fellows. Here tomorrow noon for the pay-off."

Now, the newsboys were near enough to be plainly heard. There were two of them, one on each side of the street, working toward us.

The men at the table heard and looked suddenly stricken. Brinley pushed back his chair.

"By God!" he gasped.

It was a moment to live for.

"I've got to get going," I said. "Read it and weep!"

I tore back to the city room and grabbed up a paper. It was the most beautiful sight I ever laid eyes on. The headline was big and black. It screamed: SUSPECT CAPTURED IN WENDELL MURDER!

Under it was Jetty's picture. That's how complete was our tremendous scoop. Not even the picture was lacking.

I took the paper to my desk and read every word of my story. I swelled with pride. I kept thinking, this is *my* work — every bit of it. Single-handed, I tracked down all the facts. I practically browbeat Clume into getting out the extra. I wrote every word of the story. It was even better than my paper's scoop; it was my own.

CHAPTER 18

I DREADED DOING it, but it had to be done. Mrs. Jetty was waiting for my call. Cruel as it was to tell her the truth, it would be more cruel to keep her waiting. The Nashville papers would soon get the news over their teletype and would lose no time getting in touch with her. If they didn't, she would be waiting near the telephone, listening constantly for its ring, until Jordan and Kelly walked in on her this evening.

It would be easier for her if she heard it from me. Perhaps I could soften the blow a little.

I put through the call to her and soon I heard her voice.

"Hello! Is that Mr. Reed?" And then, eagerly, "Did you find him? Is he all right?"

"Mrs. Jetty," I said, "I'm afraid I haven't very good news for you."

She gave a strangled cry as I went on, "Your husband isn't dead or injured. So far as I know, he's all right — that way. But he's in trouble here. The police have him in jail."

"In jail! What for?"

"I think it's a pretty serious charge," I replied evasively. "And listen, Mrs. Jetty, several Fairmont police officers and a reporter are on their way to see you. They'll walk in on you about seven or seven-thirty this evening. They want to question you, I suppose."

She was silent for a while.

Then she said, "Must I wait here for them? I want to get to Fairmont as quickly as possible. There's a train that leaves Nashville at five-forty and I could make it if — Must I wait?"

"There's no reason why you should," I said quickly. "You're not supposed to know they're on their way to see you. You're free to leave if you want to."

"Then I'll catch that train," she said decisively. "Mr. Reed, if you get to see my husband, will you tell him —"

"I'm afraid I won't be able to see him. I'll meet your train at the station tomorrow morning. You'll get in at seven o'clock. We'll see what can be done after you get here."

I went into Clume's office.

"Things are too good to be true," I said jubilantly. "Mrs. Jetty is going to leave Nashville on the five-forty train. When Jordan, Kelly, and that wise guy from the *Star-Herald* finish their long journey, she won't even be there. I never saw such breaks. We've got them coming and going."

Clume sighed. "I wish I weren't too old to share your illusion of victory. But perhaps it isn't my age that restrains me, but my maturity."

"Illusion of victory!" I echoed. "If this isn't a real victory, I never saw one! We made a beat that newspaper men will be talking about twenty years from now. We've won a new prestige in this town —"

"With the public or newspaper men?"

"With the public, I believe; but certainly with the newspaper men.

But that isn't all of the victory. We've shown Bruce and Cook that they can't double-cross us and get away with it. What more do you want?"

"Much more, Rufus. And what I want, I'll never gain by sticking out my tongule at my competitors or by thumbing my nose at policemen. I have a purpose, and I've always bent all my energies toward accomplishing it. But nothing that has happened today brings me any nearer my goal."

He paused a moment; then added pensively, "The murders have given me the opportunity I've waited for, for many years. But my victory may still be a long way off."

I scoffed at his pessimism. "They've got Jetty, haven't they? Now everything depends on the story he tells."

He shook his head slowly. "It's not that simple, Rufus. Let us suppose that his story puts Thomas Wendell in a bad light; that he pleads self-defense; that he declares that Wendell tried to kill him, and tells *why* Wendell tried to kill him. That he'll do that is problematical. It's a thought that may be fathered by my wish. But even if he does, the question remains: Can he prove it? Unless he has undeniable proof, nobody will believe him. The general opinion will be that he's trying to lie his way out, or that he's insane."

"There's no use in worrying about it now," I said. "Let's wait until we hear his story. I'm going to tackle the district attorney right now. We've taken the cat out of the bag, and Cook will have to come across with a statement."

In spite of Clume's dispiriting mood, my head was in the clouds as I made my way to the Criminal Courts Building. At every step I encountered evidence of the sensation I had provided. The shouts of newsboys still rang through the streets. Everyone had a copy of the paper. Standing in doorways, sitting in cars parked at the curbs, people were reading of the capture of the Wendell killer. *My* story. I had turned out a best seller.

I entered the district attorney's outer office with a jaunty step and gave frigid Miss Fleming a cheery salute.

"Good afternoon," I said. "Will you kindly inform the district attorney that a representative of the *Evening Express* prays an interview?"

"I don't have to tell him," she replied. "I know that he's very anxious to see you. You can go right in."

I pushed open the door, pausing in the frame. Cook sat at his desk, his back toward me. My heart gave a small leap when I saw a copy of the extra spread open on his desk. Across the room, at a window, stood Captain Bruce. His back was also toward me. He was looking out of the window, standing spread-legged with his hands clasped behind him.

For a moment they were unaware of my presence. Then Bruce swung around and glared at me.

"So there you are!"

Cook hitched his chair around. He glared at me, too, his lips a thin, tight line.

I gave them a smile and closed the door.

"Cheerio!" I said. "Have you heard the news?"

Cook said, "Sit down, Reed. I want to talk to you."

I sat down. He reached out and rapped the black headline with his knuckles.

"What's the meaning of this?"

"I thought that was an example of clear, forceful writing," I replied. "What don't you understand about it?"

Bruce strode toward me. His face was beet-red.

"Look here!" he shouted. "You know damn' well —"

Cook stopped him by showing him the palm of his hand.

"Let me handle this, Captain." He turned to me and said tightly, "I'm waiting for an explanation."

"If you want an explanation," I said, "I'll give you one. In other words, you're asking for it. It simmers down to this: You started it, and we finished it. We tried to shoot square with you, but you wouldn't let us. Captain Bruce will tell you that I went to his office this morning. I intended to tell him that I had traced Giles Jetty and had just returned from Jetty's farm in Tennessee. I intended to turn over to him the photograph that Mrs. Jetty gave me. We were ready to turn over a lot of valuable information that cost us time, work, and money, without first profiting by it. But we changed our minds when we found out that you were trying to double-cross us."

"What do you mean?"

"You know damn' well what I mean," I said with increasing heat. "You let a *Star-Herald* man go to Tennessee with Jordan and Kelly. Our reply to that is on your desk. How do you like it?"

Cook prided himself on never losing his temper, inside a courtroom or out of one. But I could see that he was finding it difficult to keep from hitting the ceiling. His face grew red with his effort.

"I *don't* like it. Granted that you were justified in publishing Jetty's background, there's no possible justification for deliberately publishing falsehoods. The dirtiest yellow paper in the country would hesitate to resort to such rotten tactics. This story is a lie, and you know it's a lie!"

"Just hearsay, is it?" I returned mockingly. "Only it happens that I personally got my information from reliable sources. No less than Mrs. Jetty herself."

"I'm not talking about Jetty's background. I don't know how you traced him to Tennessee, and I don't care. I'm talking about the lie that we captured the man and are secretly holding him in jail." He stopped abruptly, opened a drawer of his desk, and took out a typewritten slip of paper. "Here's my answer to that. I've given this statement to the other papers, and I demand that the *Express* publish it also. Read it!"

I took the paper and read:

The office of the district attorney-general brands as utterly false certain statements published in the *Evening Express* of this date; namely, concerning the capture and imprisonment of one Giles Jetty, sought in connection with the murder of Thomas Wendell.

This man still remains a fugitive. Whenever his capture is effected, the public will be so informed. Any statement to the contrary should be regarded by the public as misleading and unfounded on fact.

(Signed) Ben Cook
District Attorney

"What beats me," I said, folding the paper and putting it in my pocket, "is how you can have the nerve to issue a statement like that. The true facts are exactly as we published them. Giles Jetty was registered under the name of John Smith of Nashville at the Palace Hotel. On Tuesday morning he was arrested near the hotel by Peterkin and Kelly. You can't crawl out by denying it!"

"Look here!" Bruce shouted, leaning toward me across a corner of the desk. "Who told you that the man we picked up was Giles Jetty?"

"I know it," I said. "That's plenty."

"You're trying to do some smart guessing," Bruce retorted, "and you've made a damn fool of yourself! We've picked up dozens of suspects during the past week. The man you're talking about was one of them. We held him for fifteen minutes and let him go."

"Let him go!"

"Certainly. *He wasn't Giles Jetty!*"

I felt as if he had given me a smashing blow in the pit of the stomach.

I said hollowly, "But I thought — I was sure that —"

Cook saw that he had me, and he let me have it.

"I haven't had time to study this story you printed. But if you've libeled me, or Captain Bruce, or anyone else, Clume is going to pay through the nose. If there isn't any cause for a libel action, we'll smash the *Express* with it, anyway. You can't print fake news for the sensation and get away with it. You said a little while ago that we started, and you finished it. Well, you're mistaken, Reed. *We will* finish it!"

I got up shakily. There wasn't much fight left in me, but what little I had I tried to use.

"I don't know whether you're telling the truth or trying to bluff me," I said. "If you really let that man go and it turns out that you made a damn-fool mistake —"

"Mistake!" cut in Bruce. "How could we have made a mistake?"

"I don't know," I said helplessly. "But it wouldn't be the first time you pulled a boner."

He looked at me as if my stupidity were pitiful. I suppose it was.

"Don't be a sap, Red. All we had to do was check his fingerprints."

CHAPTER 19

I DIDN'T SHOW myself in the city rooom until nearly half-past five. When I left the d. a.'s office at a quarter to four, I felt that I could never again face Clume, or Boley, or even Jimmy Grant. I knew that I was through there; that I was washed up as a newspaper man. I had pulled one of those classic boners that no man could live down.

Without any destination in mind, I began to walk up one street and down another, anywhere in order to keep going. Had I kept on walking until I reached the other side of the earth, I would have been just as near to what I was running away from. After nearly an hour of aimless wandering, that thought brought me up short. I found myself on South Twenty-eighth Street, in front of Ganini's.

I went in.

Cocktail hour hadn't yet come to Fairmont. People still did their drinking at night, and Ganini's was almost empty. I went into a booth, ordered a pint of rye, and grimly set about putting it away. I didn't expect to feel any better. My purpose was to get beyond feeling at all.

When I was drinking the last of the pint, the waiter brought over a paper and without a word laid it on the table. It was a *Star-Herald*

extra, and the headline was: WENDELL KILLER CAPTURE
BRANDED FALSE. I read every word of the story which began
with Cook's statement of denial in bold-faced type. It dragged us
over the hot coals. Dispensing with the usual phrase, "an evening
paper," it called the culprit by name as Cook had done in his statement. It accused us, not of having made a natural mistake, but of
being deliberately deceptive. Such an error was too easy to avoid
to have been accidental. The police were eager to cooperate with
the press in keeping the public informed.

The man, describing himself as John Smith of Nashville, was arrested, finger-
printed, and released when it was seen that his fingerprints did not match those
which are known to belong to the fugitive, Giles Jetty. The fingerprints are, of
course, conclusive. But there were other points of difference. While it is true
that the arrested man answers somewhat the description of Jetty, and for that
reason was picked up by the police, he does not walk with a limp, an identifying
characteristic of the fugutive.
"The police hope to have Giles Jetty under arrest within 48 hours," District
Attorney Cook told a STAR-HERALD reporter this afternoon. "When he is captured, the police will know about it before the EVENING EXPRESS!"
Officials question the authenticity of the photograph published by the EX-
PRESS, purported to be that of the wanted man.
"In view of the unscrupulous hoax," Cook declared, "it may be a picture of
anybody!"

There were about three columns of it in the same vein, but that
was the part which hit me hardest. A wave of anger broke over me,
and I changed my mind about ordering a second pint and continuing
on the road to oblivion. I called for my check and hurried out to
Twenty-eighth Street where there were always taxis waiting to
carry away the casualties.

I was cold sober, but the whisky had given me courage to face the
music. I didn't slink into the city room; I walked in. The hum of
voices I heard as I came up the steps suddenly stopped. Everyone
stared at me in solemn silence. Boley, sitting at his desk with his
green eyeshade at a crazy angle, appeared to be suffering from an
attack of jaundice. Critchfield was sitting on the end of his own
desk, with his arms crossed over his chest like a martyr waiting for
martyrdom. He looked frightened and sort of worried, as if he were
trying to remember anything *he* might have done that could be held
against him.

Everybody looked at me, but no one spoke. No one except Frank
Matson, our sports editor.

As I passed his desk he said sympathetically, "Tough break, Red.
You can't hit safely every trip to the plate."

I went into Clume's office.

He sat loosely in his big armchair, his heavy square chin resting on his chest, his eyes closed. For a moment I thought he was asleep. I closed the door noiselessly and leaned back against it. As I looked at him, my alcoholic courage failed me. I was reminded not of my personal disaster but of his.

On his desk lay a copy of the *Star-Herald* extra with the entire front page exposed. I thought dismally: God! It must have hit him hard when he first laid eyes on that!

He opened his eyes, raised his head a little, and looked at me. He sniffed several times.

In his usual matter-of-fact tone he said, "I sense you haven't come alone. Have you been celebrating, Rufus?"

I had to swallow a couple of times before I could speak.

Finally I said, "Before you fire me, Mr. Clume, I — I want to tell you — well, all I can say is, I'm sorry as hell! And I don't mean for myself, either."

"Where did you get the stuff?" he asked, sniffing again. "It smells like campaign whisky. Now that you've proved that you can stand up, suppose you sit down? I've been waiting to talk to you."

I dropped into the other chair.

"I went to Ganini's intending to get stiff. I thought I couldn't come back here and take my medicine. But I changed my mind."

He sighed. "Well, you're here. I didn't expect you to start a fight and then run away. You said something about my firing you. What makes you think I'm going to let you go?"

I stared at him. There was a humorous lift to his lips, a twinkle in his eyes.

"Do you mean — I — I've still got my job?"

"Of course. I can't lay off help during the busy season. And it looks very much as though the busy season has started."

I blurted out, "Mr. Clume, you are the whitest, kindest, swellest—"

He stopped me.

"Wait, Rufus. No man was ever eulogized by a more atrocious set of adjectives, but I appreciate the tribute. However, your opinion of me differs from that of Ben Cook. He called me up and told me so."

I knotted my fists.

"I guess he demanded that you publish his statement."

He nodded.

"We can't do it!" I cried. "No after what the *Star-Herald* published. If we publicly retract anything, we'll be retracting everything. It's true that we — I mean, *I* — made a mistake about the man they picked up. But the rest of our story is correct: Jetty's background, the photograph. They said it's untrue from first to last."

"I spoke to Cook before this appeared," Clume returned. "I told him I'd give the matter serious consideration. That's what I've been doing for the past hour and a half."

"And —"

"I haven't made up my mind. Cook's statement won't be in our next edition, and we may never print it. Everything depends on — a number of things. Don't let this get you down, Rufus. We'll pull through; and maybe you'll have a better understanding of victories." Out came his big watch. "Five-thirty exactly."

He hitched back his chair. "You're meeting Mrs. Jetty at the train tomorrow? Get her a room at the General Wendell, but let her register under another name. I don't think we'll get out an extra about her arrival, though we'll be the only paper in town that will know about it."

 **CHAPTER 20**

AT THE UNION STATION next morning I learned that the train from Nashville was fifteen minutes late. I went into the waiting room, picked up a *Times* at the newsstand, and found a place on a bench. I unfolded the paper somewhat reluctantly, thinking that the feature story would be an echo of the *Star-Herald's* broadside. I was mistaken. They had plenty to say about the *Express* and its questionable methods, and Cook's statement was conspicuously reiterated on the front page; but that wasn't the feature story. The headline jerked me to attention: GHOULS VIOLATE WENDELL TOMB.

They gave it all the wordage it would bear, but, briefly, this is what happened: Early that morning a watchman at Elmwood Cemetery discovered that Wendell's vault had been broken into during the night. The bolted grille on the front of the vault had been pried away, probably with a crowbar, the casket had been pulled out, and the lid opened, but the body had not been removed. The vandals had left no clues.

I had no time to ponder this mysterious development, for just as

I was reading the last of the story, the tail of my eye glimpsed two men who passed me on their way to the train shed. I recognized them, ducked down behind the spread of my paper until they left the waiting room. They were Detective Peterkin and Jack Brinley of the *Star-Herald*.

As soon as they were out of sight, I raced outside to my parked car. It was one minute to seven and the train was fifteen minutes away. In ten minutes it would make a stop at Westside station for those passengers who wished to leave the train near the residential district.

It was interesting that Wendell's vault had been broken into, but it wasn't as interesting as the appearance of Peterkin and Brinley at Union Station at just the time when the Nashville train usually arrived. I had a hunch. Jordan, Kelly and Jimmy Nelson had reached the Jetty farm last night. They learned that Mrs. Jetty had left to take the five-forty train out of Nashville. What followed was obvious. I was surprised that neither I nor Clume had thought of it yesterday.

I stepped on the gas and reached Westside station just as the train was pulling in. I ran back to the Pullmans. Several passengers were getting off, and the conductor had swung to the platform.

"Hold it a minute," I asked him, climbing into the rear Pullman. "I'm taking off a passenger."

She wasn't in that one, but I found her in the second. She was sitting at a window with her hat on and her bag ready to be carried out. I greeted her, picked up her bag, and told her to follow me. I made no attempt to explain until we were in my car.

"I decided that you'd be more comfortable at an uptown hotel. I'll take you to the Roxborough. That isn't far from here."

She wasn't concerned about her hotel.

"I read the papers on the train, Mr. Reeed. There's a lot I don't understand. I can't make out what really happened — what's true and what isn't. He isn't in jail, as you told me on the phone, is he? But is it true, they suspect him of murder?"

As I drove, I told her everything. There was no doubt, I said, that her husband had killed Wendell. No matter how incredible it may seem, the fingerprints on the desk told the true story.

"As you read in the paper," I said, "that man at the Palace Hotel was not your husband. I thought it was, and that's why I told you he was in jail."

"But it must have been Giles!" she said miserably. "How could Sam Olden be mistaken? He was a close friend and neighbor for years."

"That's the way I figured," I replied ruefully. "I was also fooled by the name he was registered under at the hotel — John Smith of Nashville. I thought that was a give-way. But no matter how logical your conclusions seem to be, you can't stack them up against a set of fingerprints. One man may look so much like another that their own wives couldn't tell them apart, but no two fingerprints are the same."

It's hard to sell a woman an idea that she doesn't favor. Mrs. Jetty wanted to believe that Sam Olden had found her husband. She wanted the assurance that he was alive and well, even though he was charged with murder.

As I approached the Roxborough, I told her that Asaph Clume planned to back the defense of her husband whenever he was captured.

I added, "Mr. Clume wants you to register under an assumed name, so that you won't be bothered by the police or reporters. I think it would be better if I didn't go into the hotel with you. Register under the name of Mrs. James Roberts of Chicago, and stay in your room until I telephone you. It will be to your advantage to co-operate with us. We're ready to help you any way we can."

I turned her over to the Roxborough door man and drove away. As long as I kept her under cover, I had Bruce and the d. a. where I wanted them. They'd have to come to me for whatever information they had hoped to get from Mrs. Jetty. I'd give it to them only on the condition that they'd publicly acknowledge where it came from. That would certainly take the edge off Cook's statement.

I stopped off at a restaurant for breakfast, and then drove on to my parking lot near the office. As I walked into the entrance to the city room stairway, a man stepped out and took hold of my arm. It was Peterkin.

"Hello, Pete!" I said. "What are you doing around here?"

He glowered.

"Come along with me, Red. The d. a. wants to see you."

"So what?" I replied. "If he wants to see me, he can come up to the city room. I'll probably be there for the next few hours."

He held my arm, working his fingers inside the cuff of my coat.

"Do you want to come along nice, or should I call the wagon?"

"Do you mean you're arresting me?"

"I mean you're gonna come along with me to the d. a.'s office."

I shrugged.

"O. K.," I said. "But stop wrinkling that coat sleeve. What do you think I am — a dip?"

"It looks like it," he said, releasing his hold. "Or a train robber."

Bruce and Cook were waiting for me in the d. a.'s office. Bruce looked more worried than angry. I took a look at Cook's purplish face and thought: If he doesn't take his foot off his self-control brake, he's going to have a stroke.

Peterkin delivered me and went out.

Cook said, "Sit down, Reed!" and his voice sounded like a tight G-string.

I sat down, lighted a cigarette, and waited for the game to start. It was all very much like yesterday except that I now had something on the ball.

Cook asked, "Where is Mrs. Jetty?"

I looked surprised but not too surprised.

"Mrs. Jetty? Do you mean the woman I interviewed down in Tennesse last Tuesday?"

"Never mind the stalling! I know that you took her off the train this morning at Westside station. Peterkin got your description from the conductor. Where is she?"

"I don't seem to remember. In fact, I can't remember meeting any train this morning. If I think of it later, I'll let you know."

Bruce cried, "Look here, Red! You can't fool around with us! Who in hell do you think you are? You're obstructing justice!"

Cook took up the tune.

"We don't intend to waste any time with you, Reed. You will either tell us where you have concealed Mrs. Jetty, or you'll go to jail and stay there until you change your mind. Which shall it be?"

"On what charge?" I asked coolly.

"Mrs. Jetty is a material witness. If you withhold her —"

"I'm not withholding anybody," I said. "If she's in town, she is perfectly free to communicate with anyone she pleases. And you and the police are free to find out where she is and communicate with her. I don't know anything about it. Before you can get out a warrant for my arrest, you've got to prove something. And it must be something more than that I met a visitor at the train. There's nothing criminal about that."

Cook was very near the exploding point. But he managed to hold on.

He said evenly, "You know that Jordan and Kelly went to Tennessee to question that woman. You must have put her up to leaving before they got there. You also knew that Peterkin went to meet her at the station this morning. You conspired to conceal a material witness."

"How did I learn all that? You may have told the other papers but you didn't say anything to us. You're talking a lot of baloney and you know it. Now, listen, I interviewed Mrs. Jetty last Tuesday and I found out everything she knows. If you and the police aren't capable of doing what I did, it's just too bad. But in that case, you can ask me kindly to tell you what I know, and maybe I'll do it. That is, I will if you don't get too funny about it. I'll tell you on the condition that you publicly announce that your information came from a reporter on the *Express*."

Cook stared at me, his lower lip between his teeth.

"I'll see you in hell first!" he said at length. "Captain, get busy and find that woman. Search every hotel and lodging house from the roof to the basement if you have to." He turned back to me. "You can clear out of here. I realize that you're nothing but a tool for Asaph Clume. I knew you before you went to work for that fanatic, and you were an entirely different kind of man. Fundamentally, this affair is between me and Clume. You can tell him that for me."

CHAPTER 21

I DUCKED INTO the nearest telephone booth and called Mrs. James Roberts.

I said, "This is Rufus Reed. The police have learned that you're in town and they'll soon locate you there. But it's important that they don't find you right now. Please take my word for it. Leave your room immediately and walk one block east on Central Boulevard. Just leave by the same door you entered this morning. On the corner is a drug store. Go in there and wait for me. I'll call for you in less than ten minutes."

"Shall I check out — take my bag?"

"No. Keep your room. I'm going to take you to see Mr. Clume."

Twenty minutes later I escorted her into the city room. I parked her at my desk where she could not be seen from the entrance and went around to Clume's office.

He greeted me with, "I see that you obey orders at any cost." There was amusement in his tone. "When I told you to meet Mrs. Jetty, take her to a hotel, and register her under an assumed name, I didn't expect you to kidnap her. A moment ago the district attorney called me, and he seemed to be under the impression that I was the party of the first part, or perhaps the second or third part, with you and Mrs. Jetty having precedence over me. What is this conspiracy I may go to jail for? What have you done with Mrs. Jetty?"

I grinned. "I've got her outside. I couldn't leave her at a hotel because the police are searching all the hotels."

Gleefully I told him about my proposition to Cook.

"I can understand your attitude," Clume answered thoughtfully. "But there's a less hazardous way to get the same result. Get a picture of Mrs. Jetty in the city room. See that the background is unmistakable. Then notify the district attorney that you have found her and want to surrender her. Let them send here for her. Have one of the photographers on the job to take a picture of the scene when you turn her over to the officers. We can use the pictures with a story in our city edition. Would that satisfy your honor, Rufus?"

"You're the boss," I said. "I'd like to give Cook more of a runaround, but I'll do as you say."

He nodded. "The sooner, the better. I want you to be free to write an important story. I'm not sure when I'll need it."

"What about?"

"You'll learn that later. Did you read about the desecration of Wendell's vault? What do you make of it?"

"I haven't had time to give it thought. I can't see any connection —"

"Critchfield tells me that the police think it is Jetty's work. But they don't seem to ascribe any reason for the act. Perhaps —" The telephone rang and he broke off to answer it.

He listened a moment and said, "Send him in."

I had started toward the door, and he stopped me.

"Just a moment, Rufus. There's a man coming in to see me. Stay and listen."

The visitor was a short, square-shouldered young man, with sharp, shrewd features. He introduced himself as Henry Jepson, desk clerk at the Union Hotel in Arnoldburg. Arnoldburg, a town of about 70,000, is 45 miles north of Fairmont.

"I think I've got an interesting story for you," he said, getting down to business. "You pay for news, don't you?"

"It depends upon the news," Clume replied.

"Well, the news I've got is hot. It's worth a lot of money."

"What do you call a lot of money?"

"Well — a coupla hundred, anyway."

"Prices are established by supply and demand. News is one of the most plentiful of products. I might almost say that there's an over-abundance of it, so that it's a drug on the market. What kind of news do you specialize in? Perhaps you can convince me that you have the rare two-hundred-dollar variety."

"I've got it, all right," Jepson returned, his self-assurance shaken a trifle.

"That's news in itself," said Clume. "I'd like to see a sample. If I like the quality, I may give you an order."

Jepson pulled at a thatch of his straw-colored hair.

"I've heard a lot about you, Mr. Clume. I've heard that you were sort of — of — unusual. Anyway, I know I can trust you to treat me right."

"And your story?"

"Well, it's about that fellow, Giles Jetty, that the cops are looking for."

Clume's face remained unchanged. "Yes?"

"I know something about him."

"Why don't you give your information to the police?"

"That's it. I don't want to give it; I want to sell it. I wouldn't get so much as a thank-you from the cops. You see, I read your extra when it came to Arnoldburg last night. As soon as I saw that guy's picture, I recognized him. He stopped at my hotel for over two weeks."

"When?"

"He checked in on October 8th, and he checked out on October 25th. He was with us all that time. Of course, I read all about Mr. Wendell's murder and about the cops looking for a man named Giles Jetty, but somehow, that name didn't click with me. But when I looked at his picture last night, I remembered him. I remembered that he was the fellow who checked in on the morning of the eighth, went to his room, and stayed there nearly all day, without even going out to lunch. A chambermaid told me he was spending the whole time writing a letter. She went in several times to bring in towels, etc. Along about four in the afternoon, he came down to the desk and asked me to weigh a letter for him and sell him the right amount of stamps. It was a thick letter, and he wanted to send it special delivery, registered. I told him he'd have to take it to the post office."

"Did you see the address?"

"No. I didn't take the letter when he said it was going to be registered. Anyway, from the next day on he just stuck around the hotel, staying in his room most of the time, but coming to the desk every time the mail came in, and a few times in between. The only thing I ever heard him say was, 'Is there a letter for me?' That man wanted a letter and he wanted it bad. On the morning of the twenty-fifth, he checked out."

Clume listened, his thumb and forefinger traveling up and down his nose.

When Jepson paused, he asked, "Is that all?"

"All? That's only the introduction. I'm getting to the proof that the man I'm talking about is really Giles Jetty. Look here. I got his register card out of our files. Here it is. 'Giles Jetty, Franklin, Tennessee; written in his own hand. Kind of shaky, ain't it? He wrote very slow, like it was a tough job. I guess that's why it took him nearly all day to write a long letter. But now let me tell you the real story. I —"

"Just a moment, Mr. Jepson. You say that this man came to your hotel on October 8th. Well, this card proves the date. But can you prove that he was there all the next day — on the ninth?"

"I sure can. I don't think he even stepped out of the hotel all that day, and I'm positive he wasn't out as long as half an hour at any time."

"All right. Now what's the rest of the story?"

"Well, the real important news is that I know where he is right now."

I jumped to my feet.

"Where is he?"

"Sit down, Rufus," Clume said. "Let's hear what Mr. Jepson has to say."

"He's at another hotel in Arnoldburg," said Jepson. "Last night, after I finished reading the paper, I saw him walking along the street. I tailed him to the Hotel Keene. I learned from their clerk that he was registered under the name of William Jetts from Nashville, Tennessee. He checked in early Wednesday morning. Before I left this morning, I found out he was still there."

Clume sat up a little straighter in his chair, opened a desk drawer, and took out a checkbook.

"Your story," he said, reaching for a pen, "is more interesting than I expected." He wrote a check, tore it out of the book, and handed it to Jepson. "Here's a check for two hundred dollars. It includes payment for this registration card and for your willingness to repeat your story under oath if or when the occasion arises. Is that agreed?"

Jepson, his face shining, folded the check.

"It sure is, Mr. Clume. Anything you say."

"Excellent. Now I'll ask you to wait outside in the city room for a few minutes, and we'll see what is to be done. Rufus, remain a while."

When the door closed on Jepson, I said, "I know you think his story is straight, or you wouldn't have handed over that check."

"Of course it's straight. And you recognize its importance, don't you? I mean, aside from the fact that we can get hold of him, if he doesn't move on before we can get there. Consider these points: He registered at the Union Hotel in Arnoldburg on Sunday, October 8th. He was there on Monday, October 9th."

"Which means that he couldn't have killed Vincent Creel."

"Certainly. He left Arnoldburg on the morning of October 25th. At five o'clock that afternoon, Wendell was murdered." His eyes were glowing. "He returned to Arnoldburg Wednesday morning and was still there this morning. That means that it wasn't Jetty who broke into Wendell's vault. It also means that we have everything we need and are ready to go."

He reached for a cigarette like a hungry man, and I held a match for him. He was as near to being excited as I've ever seen him.

"Rufus, get my car out of the garage. It's roomier and faster than yours. Take Jepson and Mrs. Jetty with you and go to Arnoldburg. As long as Mrs. Jetty is with you, you should have no trouble persuading Jetty to return peaceably. This case is just about closed."

 **CHAPTER 22**

JEPSON WAS TO come back with us, so he left his car and rode with us. He and Mrs. Jetty sat on the rear seat, and I took the wheel. There was the usual delay getting out of the city, but once I struck the open road, I clipped off the remaining forty miles in almost that many minutes.

When we got to Hotel Keene in Arnoldburg, Jepson remained in the car; and Mrs. Jetty and I went in. She was game and holding up admirably.

As we entered the hotel, she said to me, "It's wonderful to find him, even if we — if we —"

"Don't you worry, Mrs. Jetty. There's a lot we don't understand that he can tell us. But we'll get him out of this."

I went to the desk and asked for William Jetts. I waited nervously while they rang his room telephone.

The clerk said, "He doesn't answer."

"Isn't he in his room?"

"He doesn't seem to be. But his key isn't down here."

I said, "I'm with his wife and it's very important that we see him right away. Can't we go up and knock on his door?"

He looked me over.

"I guess you can. I'll send a boy up with you." He tapped a bell. "Is there something wrong with the man?"

"Wrong? What do you mean?"

"Well —" He hesitated. "I mean, is he perfectly normal? I thought he acted kind of peculiar. Like he was in a daze."

"He was shell-shocked in the war," I said. "He gets those spells. That's why I brought his wife to him."

The bell hop took us to the elevator, and we went up to the fourth floor. The boy knocked on the door, and when there was no answer, he knocked again. I took a dollar bill out of my pocket and put it in the boy's hand.

"Let's open the door and have a look. Have you got a key?"

"I can get one."

"O.K. We'll wait."

He came back a few minutes later with a ring of keys. I stood close to Mrs. Jetty, holding her arm. I could feel her trembling.

As soon as the door was opened, we saw that we were too late. Even before we took a step into the room, we saw him stretched out on the bed. He didn't look like a man asleep. He looked like a dead man.

Five minutes later, I was talking to Clume over the telephone. I was phoning in a story, and that's the way I let him have it — just the bare facts that could be whipped into a story and rushed into an extra: found dead in room 414 at the Hotel Keene; suicide; slashed wrist with razor blade; probably been dead since last night; body cold; Mrs. Jetty holding up well; she will remain with the body until Fairmont police arrive.

Just before I hung up, I said, "That's all, Mr. Clume. That gives us a scoop that makes up for what happened yesterday. And that's all we *will* get out of it!"

The Arnoldburg cops were considerate of Mrs. William Jetts, the suicide's widow. They didn't question her any more than they had to. They gave her a room at the hotel and let her alone with her grief while I made arrangements with an undertaker for the removal of the body to his establishment. I passed myself off as Mrs. Jett's nephew.

Assured that everything was safe, I put Jepson in the car and started back to Fairmont. He was talkative at first, but when he saw that I wasn't listening, he fell silent and left me to my thoughts. They weren't pleasant. We had reached the end of a long, hard road, and all that we got for our trouble was a scoop on the *Star-Herald*. I knew what Clume thought of scoops. It wasn't his idea of victory, and now, somehow or other, it wasn't my idea, either.

I was about eight miles out of Fairmont when a tire blew out. There was a gas-service station about fifty yards up the road, so I left Jepson in the car and walked ahead. I told the attendant I wanted a tire changed, and he sent a colored man with the trouble-truck.

I was about to climb into the truck for a ride back when the attendant asked, "Which way were you goin'? Did you just leave Fairmont?"

"I'm on my way there."

"Boy! I'll bet there's plenty excitement in town!" he said. "Wonder what'll come of it?"

"Have you seen an extra?" I asked quickly.

"Yeh. A fellow brought it in from town ten minutes ago."

I jumped out of the truck.

"I want to see it," I said. "I'll look it over while I'm waiting."

"Sure. Help yourself. It's in there on the desk."

I went into the office and grabbed up the green-fronted paper. It was lucky that there was a chair right under me, for the shock knocked my legs from under me. I dropped heavily upon that chair, gaping at the astonishing headline. It didn't say anything about Jetty's suicide; Jetty's name wasn't in it. The headline shouted: THOMAS WENDELL ACCUSED OF MURDER!

I passed my hand over my eyes and looked again. It was still there, shouting the same thing. I felt that I had seen that headline before; and then I remembered that it was the one Clume had wanted to print six days after Creel's murder. Now, three weeks later, here it was!

Stunned by surprise, I looked at that front page. At the left, a short, two-column story set in heavy black type, told of Jetty's suicide. In the center, columns 4, 5 and 6 were merged in a box that ran the full length of the page, and this story was set in 12-point. At the top was the startling head, Murder Will Out! At the foot it was signed, "Asaph Clume, Publisher of THE EVENING EXPRESS."

It was written in the form of an editorial, and the gist of it was this; that Thomas Wendell, once accused by Mrs. Oliver Embry of the murder of Vincent Creel and carelessly absolved by the police, was actually guilty of the crime.

It was a flat, bald statement, unadorned by any attempts at proof, and the editorial went on as if the statement must be accepted as fact. In view of Wendell's guilt, the Embrys were completely vindicated. How unjust their persecution had been! But was not injustice to be expected under the evil conditions that existed in Fairmont? The Embrys had been crushed by the Juggernaut driven by Thomas Wendell — "driven by Thomas Wendell, the murderer, with the consent of a blinded public."

The rest of the long editorial was political in character, exhorting the people to be blind no longer, to worship false gods no longer, to rise up and overthrow the graven images, to reestablish and avenge the pitiful Embry family whose case typified the blight which had fallen upon the entire community.

As I read, the sweat came out on my face and body. I didn't need a lawyer to point out a libelous phrase. It was all libelous.

I drove to Fairmont in a daze. I let Jepson out of the car at the parking lot, asked him to phone me at the office at three o'clock when I'd be able to tell him whether or not we'd need him, and went to the office.

As soon as I entered the city room, I perceived that I was not the only one who was stunned. The atmosphere was almost as thick with gloom as it had been yesterday afternoon.

Boley called me to his desk and asked, "Red, do you know what's behind all this?"

"No," I said. "I read it out on the road and I damn' near dropped dead. All I expected was an extra about Jetty's death."

"You mean to tell me that you haven't any proof that Wendell killed Creel?

"Not a shred. It's pure guess-work."

"Maybe he has proof," Boley said, "and he hasn't told you. I can't believe that he'd print anything like that unless he could back it up with black-and-white evidence. Not Clume."

"I hope you're right," I replied. "I'm going in and find out."

When I opened the door to his office, I saw Clume at his desk writing at a great rate. I started to back out, but he looked up.

"Come in, Rufus!"

"If you're busy —"

"I can finish this later," he said, returning his pencil to the pottery cup, gathering his papers, and putting them into a drawer. "I've finished a second editorial for a late afternoon edition. The one I'm writing is for tomorrow. I plan to run two front page editorials a day; tomorrow, Sunday, and Monday. We'll get out a special edition Sunday afternoon. We should have the voters in the right frame of mind for Tuesday's election. Tuesday night the writing on the wall should be very clear. This election can't smash the Wendell machine, but it will very definitely indicate what will happen next year."

I looked for an aberrant gleam in his eye and failed to find it.

"I suppose you have legal proof that Wendell murdered Creel. I didn't see any in that editorial of yours."

"I omitted that," he returned, "for the very simple reason that I have none."

"You can't prove it?"

"Not in the legal sense of the word," he admitted. "The murder of Creel, as you have learned by this time, is a most unusual affair. The only thing that can be considered in the nature of direct evidence is Mrs. Embry's testimony. In law, the testimony of a single eyewitness is very weak. The credibility of the witness is open to attack. Such testimony is valuable only in relation to corroborative evidence."

"Circumstantial?"

"Well, that helps; but as a general rule, circumstantial evidence is questionable. Unfortunately, all the proof we have that Wendell murdered Creel is Mrs. Embry's unsupported testimony and circumstantial evidence."

I could scarcely believe my ears. My worst fears were justified. He had no real proof that Wendell had committed murder!

"How do you expect to get away with it? I know that Wendell is dead, and *he* can't hit back. But what about Mrs. Wendell? And what about your accusations against Cook and Bruce and the whole police department? You hit right and left, and now you say you can't back up any of it with proof."

"I think I dealt quite leniently with the district attorney and the police department," he answered quietly. "It pointed out that under the present regime even capable officials lost their value to the community. Cook is an excellent lawyer. Bruce is an efficient police officer. Under a different rule, they'd serve well."

"Don't kid yourself," I said. "They aren't going to take it as a compliment. They'll make you eat your words. And it doesn't look as if you can digest them. Since you can't prove that Wendell killed Creel, you have libeled them by attacking their efficiency in this particular case."

"Let's worry about that later," he replied. "You and I know that Wendell murdered Creel in cold blood, don't we?"

"I don't know anything of the kind. All I know is that you *said* he did. You haven't any more proof of it than you had three weeks ago. You can't even show that the two men ever knew each other —"

"They didn't. I'm convinced of that. They never laid eyes on each other nor even heard of each other until that fatal afternoon. They never spoke to each other except the two words that Wendell uttered, 'Hey, there!' when he stopped his car near Mrs. Embry's house."

"And yet you expect anyone to believe that Wendell killed him!"

He did not answer that directly.

"You agree, Rufus, that there cannot be murder without motive. The difficulty of establishing Wendell's guilt has been that there was seemingly no motive for the crime. But when a man is shot to death and the possibility of suicide is precluded, we know empirically that it is murder and that, therefore, there must be a murderer. And since there is a murderer, there must be a motive, even though we fail to detect it."

"You told me yesterday," I said, "that Wendell's motive was fear. But you were talking about Wendell and Jetty. What about Wendell and Creel? Why should he fear a man he didn't know and who didn't know him? Creel was in town only —"

"Only a few minutes," he finished. "But that was long enough. We have all the pieces to the puzzle, Rufus, and we can put them together. Consider: On the afternoon of October ninth, Wendell remained in his office until a quarter past five. Before leaving, he asked his secretary, Hammond, for some money. Hammond gave him one hundred dollars in small bills. Wendell put the bills in his wallet and dropped the wallet into the side pocket of his overcoat. He went downstairs where the girl at the information desk gave him the keys to his automobile. The car was parked near the entrance to the building. He probably dropped the keys into his overcoat pocket and walked out of the building to the sidewalk and across the walk to his car.

"Now let us leave Wendell for a moment and give our attention to Vincent Creel. He had just arrived in town, hungry and broke. He and his brother have separated with the agreement to meet on the corner of Ninth and Broadway at eight o'clock. Creel stands on the corner a moment, giving his brother time to put a little distance between them. Then he follows after, walking toward Tenth Street.

"As he passes a point near the entrance to the Wendell Building, he sees a man standing at the side of an automobile at the curb. The man is facing the side of the car. He reaches into his pocket and takes out his automobile keys, inserts one into the lock of the door. That, of course, does not interest the hungry tramp. What does interest him is the fact that when the man withdrew his hand from his pocket, a wallet dropped to the sidewalk behind him. Creel pauses, and I imagine that his heart skips a beat. For the owner of the wallet doesn't seem to know he dropped it. He unlocks the car door, opens it, and gets into the car.

"The wallet is lying almost at Creel's feet. He stoops quickly, picks it up, and drops it into his own pocket. And at that instant, he notes that the man in the automobile has glanced at him. He sees the man reach quickly into his overcoat pocket.

"Creel turns and walks quickly away toward the corner from which he came. He would like to lose himself in a crowd, but the street is not very crowded. He ventures a backward glance and sees that the owner of the wallet is getting out of the car.

"At the corner is a cigar store. Here is a temporary refuge. He goes in, hoping that the man does not see him. At the rear of the store are telephone booths. He enters one.

"Now, mark this, Rufus: We know that he remained in that booth for about five minutes. He was hiding, of course, but he was not merely standing there. The clerk told you that he seemed to be studying something that he held in his hands. He was not writing that message on the telephone book; he had no pencil with him. At the end of about five minutes, he left the booth, asked the clerk for the loan of a pencil, and reentered the booth to write the message. Now what was he doing during that first stay in the booth? He was, of course, examining his lucky find. It would take him no more than one minute to count the money and separate the smallest of the bills, which happened to be five dollars. It would take hardly more than another minute for him to look through the wallet for cards and so forth which would identify the owner. Obviously he must have found in the wallet something that required a longer interval to read. What was it?

"Now we'll leave Creel for a moment and transfer our interest to Arnoldburg. It is Sunday, October eighth. Giles Jetty, who disappeared from his home some two weeks earlier, shows up at Arnoldburg, a city close to Fairmont. He goes to the Union Hotel, registering under his own name, remember, and spends many hours writing a long letter which he mails that evening, sending it special delivery, registered. I am so certain that the letter was addressed to Thomas Wendell that I have not bothered to investigate at the post office. I have no doubt that the records will show that a letter was delivered to Wendell at his office on Monday morning, and that the sender was Giles Jetty at the Union Hotel in Arnoldburg.

"It was that letter which Creel read in the telephone booth. Wendell had put it in his wallet for safe keeping. And it must have contained information that led to everything that followed. In the first place, it rendered helpless a man who knew no such thing as helplessness. Wendell saw Creel dart into the cigar store. Why didn't he go in and demand the return of his property? Why didn't he call the traffic policeman and have the tramp arrested? Because he didn't dare. He saw through the doorway that the tramp was reading something in that booth, and Wendell knew what he was reading. He was at that moment helpless through fear. There was some dangerous secret which he had thought no one else shared. The letter told him that one other man shared it. Now he could see that the tramp also shared it. That's why he made no attempt to corner the tramp in the cigar store.

"For his part, Creel realized that he had found a great deal more than one hundred dollars. He knew that he could return the pocketbook and its contents to the owner for an unlimited sum. His dream of easy riches had actually come true. So he wrote that message for his brother; and then he left the booth and returned the pencil to the clerk. As he turned away, he saw the owner of the wallet standing in the doorway to the store. He didn't realize that the man didn't dare to collar him. He saw the bus that was stopped in front of the store and he made a dash for it. His only idea was to get away from there. He should have remained where he was. He sought safety and he rode to meet death. It was his appointment in Samarra.

"For Wendell promptly got into his car and followed the bus. At the end of the line, he followed the tramp. There was only one thing to do, and he did it. He shot the tramp to death and recovered not only his wallet and its contents, but also his freedom from the tramp's knowledge. Mrs. Embry said that after he shot the tramp, he turned him over on his back and knelt beside the body as if to determine whether he was dead. He would not have to turn him over on his back to determine that. I reasoned all along that he must have taken something from the tramp's pocket. Now we know that it was his wallet containing Jetty's letter."

He stopped and looked at me.

I said unsteadily, "Mr. Clume, you've convinced me. That picture is absolutely complete. It's made up of nothing but the facts as we know them to be true. And now I know that you've been kidding me and trying to throw a scare into me. You've got proof!"

"What kind of proof?"

"Somehow or other you got hold of the letter that Jetty wrote to Wendell. You've been holding out on me!"

Slowly he shook his head.

"No, Rufus. I'm sure that the letter is no longer in existence. Wendell made a grave mistake when he failed to destroy it the very moment he read it. I suppose he wanted to take it home and ponder it that evening while he decided what to do about it. I'm sure that he wouldn't have made the mistake a second time, after he recovered it at the expense of committing murder. Unquestionably, he destroyed every trace of it the moment he reached home."

I became alarmed again.

"But if you haven't got the letter, how can you prove what happened?"

"I can't prove it, except circumstantially. As for the contents of that letter —"

The telephone bell shrilled so suddenly that I jumped. My nerves were on edge. Clume reached for his phone and said something about letting them come in. Then he settled back in his chair.

"We're about to be honored, Rufus. The district attorney is calling on us in person — and also Captain Bruce."

The door opened, and they entered, Cook in the lead.

I got up and closed the door after them while Clume said cordially, "Gentlemen, this is a pleasure. Won't you be seated? Rufus, please relieve the gentlemen of their hats."

Cook grabbed the chair nearest Clume, sitting down and thrusting his face forward aggressively.

"Never mind the nonsense, Clume! You've reached the end of your rope!"

"That's right, Cook," Clume replied. "And at the end of my rope is a noose. It is merely a question of who shall be hanged with it."

"There's no question about *that!*"

"No, I don't believe there is. The victims are marked."

Cook's masterly self-control was gone. His face was livid with rage; his voice shook with emotion. I didn't look at Bruce; I was too busy watching the d. a.

"You've been trying hard to make a sensation, Clume. Well, you have succeeded in making one, and like the Frankenstein monster —"

"Oh, come!" Clume interrupted in his weary voice. "Those rhetorical flourishes are all right in a political speech or an editorial, but they just clutter up a general conversation. Frankenstein monsters have never troubled me. Political monsters do. The victims of the noose at the end of my rope are the political monsters — Or did you come to discuss something other than politics?"

"You know what you're in for, don't you?"

"Well, yes. I'm in for an extended period, I hope. I've been out for thirteen years and now I'm going to be in again."

Cook decided to have his say and give Clume as little opportunity as possible to talk.

"Mrs. Wendell will immediately start proceedings against you. I intend to bring suit also. And Captain Bruce —"

Clume looked at Bruce, somewhat reproachfully.

"You too, Captain?"

Bruce said, "I've got to do something!"

"Don't worry, Captain," Clume said gently. "There should be plenty for you to do." He returned his attention to the district attorney. "I'm disappointed, Cook. I thought you had come to talk over a criminal case and I find you discussing civil actions. I can't be bothered. Everything of that nature I turn over to my attorney."

"You'll be bothered plenty about this!" Cook shouted. "I always knew you were eccentric. Now I'm beginning to believe you are insane. What is behind the statements you published in that editorial?"   ·

"The truth."

"Can you prove that your statements are true?"

"I believe I can."

"You have proof that Thomas Wendell murdered Vincent Creel? That is your accusation."

Clume stroked his nose.

"Not proof as you lawyers know it. Nothing that definite. Nothing that you can frame and hang on the wall of your office."

"In other words, you can't *prove* it! You have published the flat statement that Wendell is a murderer, and that I failed in my duty by not prosecuting him on the strength of Mrs. Embry's accusation. And you can *prove* nothing."

"I can offer legal proof that he killed Creel," Clume repeated levely. "But I don't believe that such proof will be necessary."

Cook raised his lip to show his upper teeth.

"Oh, you don't! But the court will think it's necessary."

"Now, now," said Clume. "Let us stick to the criminal case and leave the civil actions to the future. I'm addressing you in your capacity as district attorney. Have you brought Jetty's body from Arnoldburg?"

"Of course!"

"Are you sure you have the right man? The man you've been looking for?"

Cook's face went blank with surprise.

"I don't know what you're talking about. Of course we have the right man."

"How do you know that?"

"Why — his wife identified the body as that of her husband."

"Would you call that legal proof of his identity? Mrs. Embry, you will remember, identified Wendell as the murderer of Creel. But that isn't legal proof. You and I both like our evidence to be incontrovertible; fingerprints, for example. Have you checked the fingerprints?"

The district attorney looked harassed.

"We haven't yet. The body just came in a few minutes before I left the office. But all of this is beside the point. You are trying to cloud the issue."

"I'm trying to clarify it," said Clume. "I am reminding you that you have overlooked your own insistence upon legal proof. I ask you again: Are you *sure* that you have the body of the right man?"

Cook started to say "yes" but checked himself. Clume had him on that legal proof business, and he knew it. He knew that he was right, but he couldn't come out and say so. He hesitated an instant; then reached savagely for the telephone. He gave the number of the police station and asked to speak to Sergeant Wilcox.

"Hello, Wilcox? This is Cook speaking. I want you to take the fingerprints of Giles Jetty and compare them with the record. It's just a formality but — What's that? You did?"

He stopped speaking and listened. He listened for what seemed to me a very long time. And as he listened a strange expression came over his face. His eyes widened and protruded a little; his nostrils quivered; his mouth fell open so that the jaw sagged. The blurred buzz of Wilcox' voice in the receiver stopped.

Then Cook said in a hollow tone, "All right. We — we'll see about that later. I'll be over there shortly."

Slowly he took the receiver from his ear. Slowly he replaced it on the hook. Slowly he pushed the phone away. Slowly he turned his bewildered eyes to meet Bruce's questioning ones.

He said softly, "Wilcox took the fingerprints. They don't check."
Bruce got to his feet.

"They don't check!"

"Not with Jetty's. They're the same as the man we picked up the other day — the man at the Palace Hotel."

CHAPTER 23

FOR A LONG moment the office seemed to be deserted, so soundless did it become. No one spoke; no one moved. We were suddenly changed into grotesque statues, frozen to immobility. The unexpected struck us a paralyzing blow, stopping our mental and physical processes. When I say "us," I mean Cook, Bruce, and myself. Clume broke the spell with a single word, spoken in a mocking tone.

"Tableau!"

As if that were a cue in an animal act, all of us turned to look at him. Cook was first to find his voice, and it was a weak voice, shorn of belligerency. He asked a question in a tone that pleaded for an answer.

"Mr. Clume, what does this mean?"

Bruce had dropped back into his chair. He pulled a handkerchief from his pocket and vigorously wiped his face with it.

"It means," Clume replied, "that as a representative of justice you must be more than ordinarily careful about reaching conclusions. You are a youngish man, Cook, and you've hardly had time to be tempered by adversity. Ability and good fortune have combined to make you over-confident. Please accept this counsel in the spirit I offer it. Our relationship has been anything but friendly. But I make allowances for that. I've reached an age where my blood has cooled. Enthusiasm or intolerance can no longer warp my judgment or understanding. Circumstances put us into opposite camps, but that doesn't keep me from recognizing your potentialities."

Cook shifted uneasily in his chair, but he kept his eyes attentively on Clume's.

"I don't want to bore you with a paternal lecture," Clume went on; "but this will lay the foundation for our future relationship. Within the next twenty-four hours, I am going to smash the old machine. But whatever good pieces are lying around I want to pick up and salvage. I don't doubt your honesty or sincerity any more than I doubt the honesty and sincerity of the thousands of voters who did Thomas Wendell's bidding for thirteen years. You and they weren't corrupt. You were only mistaken."

The district attorney could stand it no longer.

He said somewhat plaintively, "I appreciate what you're saying. I really do. But you will understand —"

"Of course. But you might have spared yourself this bewilderment if you and Captain Bruce had painstakingly assembled all the facts as you would have done in any other murder case. You were unreasonably positive that Wendell couldn't have been a murderer, just as you were unreasonably positive that the fingerprints of this man who was brought from Arnoldburg would check with those of Giles Jetty. Well, what do you think now?"

"That we have the wrong man, of course." He added suddenly: "But *you* led us to him! It was through your extra —"

The corners of Clume's mouth twitched. He found this situation to his liking. He raised himself a little in his chair, opened the center drawer of his desk, and took out two slips of paper. One was a small oblong and from where I sat I couldn't see what was on it. The other was the police circular issued to aid the search for Jetty. There was no photograph, but a description was given; and there was a reproduction of the fugitive's fingerprints. Clume handed the circular to Cook. Then he handed over the second paper and a small magnifying glass. When Cook held it, I could see that the smaller paper bore two lines of fingerprints.

"Compare those prints," Clume said. *"They* check, don't they?"

Cook looked carefully through the glass, holding the two sets of fingerprints so that he could see them together. After a moment he passed the glass and the papers to Bruce.

"They check all right! Look at them, Captain!"

Bruce studied them.

"They check all right!" he echoed.

"That's evident," said Clume, "even to one as inexpert as I am. Those are Jetty's fingerprints on that slip of paper. I got them without his knowledge or consent, but I got them. While you were seeking the man, I found him, if you'll pardon my putting it so boastfully."

"Where is he?" cried the d. a.

But Clume was not to be hurried.

He said slowly, "To answer that question, I must confess to a crime. I won't ask immunity, but I feel certain that I'll be given it.

You gentlemen are looking for the vandal who opened Thomas Wendell's vault last night. I'm the man!"

"You!"

Clume nodded.

"That's where I got those fingerprints. And that answers your question as to the whereabouts of Giles Jetty. He's lying in Thomas Wendell's coffin!"

The chimes of St. Thomas were tolling the noon hour when the district attorney and Captain Bruce left the office. In his leisurely but methodical way, Clume had cleared away the last strands of the cobweb. He had gone over the case point by point, and although much of the story was, as he said, "synthetized," he left no doubt as to its factual truth.

"The fingerprints have the last word," he said in conclusion, "and they tell us as much as we need to know. Their silent testimony is incontrovertible. Giles Jetty was the man we accepted as Thomas Wendell, and Thomas Wendell was the amnesic, shell-shocked farmer who, until one morning last September, thought that he was Giles Jetty.

"We know that there was an exchange of identities, but exactly how it was brought about we can only imagine. However, this morning I spoke over long-distance with a friend in the War Department at Washington. I learned this much; that both Wendell and Jetty were members of the same regiment in France for a period of six weeks. They fought together in several battles, and, as we know, both were wounded; Wendell, the more seriously.

"Before sailing to France, Wendell had heard from his uncle Arnold; so he knew that after the war was over he would join his uncle in Fairmont and would some day inherit the Wendell fortune. If Jetty was a buddy of his in the trenches, it is natural that he'd tell of this as well as the circumstances that preceded his reinstatement into the Wendell family.

"They were probably together on the battlefield when Wendell received his wound. Jetty, believing that Wendell was done for, took advantage of the opportunity presented him. He exchanged identification tags and any papers that were in their pockets. He knew that Thomas Wendell had never been in Fairmont and had never seen his uncle. Circumstances were in his favor. He was an opportunist. We saw that during the years we knew him as Thomas Wendell.

"When he made the exchange on the battlefield, he may not have had any definite plans for the future. He would trust to luck and see what happened. Well, we know what happened. He was wounded, perhaps that very day, and taken to a hospital behind the lines. As Thomas Wendell he lay in that hospital and others until the war was over; then he was returned to the States and sent to the hospital where the executors of Arnold Wendell's estate found him.

"Beyond exchanging tags and papers with Thomas Wendell, Jetty did nothing to establish himself as the heir. He didn't have to. The Army Department directed the executors to him and they never doubted that he was the right man. His papers were in order; and among them was the letter from Arnold Wendell. He had only to accept what was handed to him, confident that the real Thomas Wendell was dead and buried in France.

"I believe that is the way it happened, but I can't offer you any legal proof. We have proof of the fact but not of the act." He paused and added, "It was Rufus' fondness for scoops that gave me the key to the riddle. As you know, I believed from the beginning that Wendell murdered Creel. I believed it because I believed Mrs. Embry. But until yesterday afternoon I didn't come anywhere near guessing the motive. After all, this case was not a matter of finding the criminal but of finding his motive, and I could think of none.

"But when I read the *Star-Herald's* extra yesterday afternoon, I saw the light. I was sure that the man you captured and released was Giles Jetty, just as Rufus had been sure of it. The fact that his fingerprints didn't check with Jetty's meant only one thing to me; that it wasn't he who left his bloody fingerprints on the desk. And if those prints didn't belong to him, they must be Wendell's. With that thought I had my answer. I had only to prove it." He pointed a long finger at the oblong slip of paper that lay on his desk. "I did."

I left with Bruce and the d. a. I had to be on the job when Mrs. Jetty was informed that she was not Mrs. Jetty but the widow of Thomas Wendell and the mistress of the Wendell fortune. On the way out of the city room I picked up a photographer and took him along with us. The story was going to be another beat for us. Cook and Bruce granted that unbegrudgingly.

As we went down the stairs, I told them, "I'm going to write this story myself and I'm going to give you fellows every possible break."

Bruce laid his big paw on my arm and said, "I'll remember it, Red," the way a kid says, "You know me, Jimmy!" when Jimmy appears with a bag of jelly beans.

At the foot of the stairs, I met Margaret Embry just coming into the entrance. She was dressed as cute as the dickens, with a trick hat on her blond curls and a dark blue knitted suit under her fur-collared coat. She looked prettier than I had ever seen her. The brooding sadness had left her face, and a glow of happiness made her beautiful.

At sight of Cook and Bruce, her face clouded for an instant, but they swished off their hats and greeted her like two young blades on the make.

I said, "Gee, Peggy, I'm glad to see you! I can tell that you've been reading the paper this morning."

She uttered a laugh that matched the rest of her.

"Isn't it simply wonderful? I was just coming to see you and Mr. Clume to — to celebrate with you."

"I'm off on a story," I said; "but you go on up and see the boss. I'll be back in a little while. How's the family?"

"Wonderful! You can imagine!"

"Did you find a job?"

"No, but I'll have one pretty soon. And so will Dad. After that editorial came out, a lot of men telephoned us and offered all sorts of jobs. I never saw such an effective want-ad!" she laughed musically. "One crank was looking for a wife!"

I said, "Don't accept right away. I want a date with you first."

"You'll have it. Mother wants to have you and Mr. Clume for dinner tonight. Do you think he'll accept?"

"Try to keep him away," I told her.

Bruce and the d. a. had come on foot, and we walked back to Cook's office where the new Mrs. Wendell was waiting. On the way we passed Bernie's, and I remembered that I had a date there at this very moment.

I said, "Fellows, you walk on and I'll catch up with you. I want to go in here a minute. I won't be long. My dark horse came in first, and I want to collect a hundred and five bucks!"

www.ingramcontent.com/pod-product-compliance
Lightning Source LLC
Chambersburg PA
CBHW050803250626
47155CB00005B/2186